Doppleganger

S. L. Phanes

Doppleganger
S. L. Phanes

ISBN: 979-8-9898008-2-7

Cover Design: S. L. Phanes

This story is dedicated to innocence.
Innocence lost and innocence reborn.

Contents

History

As children, Oasis and I revered her father as a hero. When he and his husband, John Gabriel Utterson, passed away, they left us their legacy: The institute of Lysology. It was then that we reached a different conclusion.

Dr. Henry Jekyll was far from a hero. Instead, he was a scientist driven by an insatiable hunger for discovery. His research with the formula he created failed in London, and John had dragged his poisoned body to Dr. Amy. After addressing Henry's ailment, she urged both of them to leave London because the Carews had no intention of leaving them alone. They moved to Runeburgh, where I arrived as a nine-year-old boy—alone, famished, and cold. Why am I sharing this with you?

Because my name is Elliot Warlow, and you must understand the complexity of my history, our shared history, and the history of Lysology. It is this very history and its progression that now leads me and Oasis to accept Anthony Carew's invitation to Runeburgh's annual Science and Development Ceremony.

The last time they invited the institute was nine

years ago.

Oasis and I have struggled to keep the institute afloat for five years now, teaching any psychology courses at the University of Runeburgh to ensure our survival and preserve our history.

I detest Anthony Carew's smug expression and self-satisfied grin. Oasis and I have refused to welcome him into our institute since 1921, the year John and Henry passed away. But our history and legacy were in jeopardy, little did I know my livelihood, very soul, were at stake, as well.

Revision

Jekyll had created the institute of Lysology with the hopes of researching the soul through his formula. After extensive research in Runeburgh, before the Council halted his work, Dr. Jekyll realized he had been mistaken all along. You know the story—human nature is not singular, but dual, composed of good and evil. Jekyll sought to separate these opposing forces within himself.

It was too late when he discovered he could not eliminate one without destroying the other, let alone separate the two. Hence, the name of this institute: Lysology is the study of the release of the soul, not the separation from it, through the process called Shifting. He never understood how to achieve safe Shifting, and he died without finding the answer.

Oasis had a well-founded theory. If accepted at the Ceremony, this theory would advance the field of Lysology and would further our understanding of the human soul. That was our hope. "Runeburgh's entire scientific community will undoubtedly reject this theory," Oasis said. She measured 0.5 grams of Nafs, new salts to replace those Jekyll once used in his formula.

She combined 1 milliliter of autolysine and 4 milliliters of catalyst with 10 milliliters of solvent. I placed it on the Bunsen burner, and it bubbled slightly. "I believe Edward Hyde was my father's soul—or at least the discarded part of it." Oasis turned up the heat, and the solution dissolved, bubbling furiously. It transformed from the emerald green of the salts to a fleeting amethyst purple before settling on a deep crimson red. "If this formula is successful, we can safely release your soul through it. This would provide a tangible, safer Shifting process and a better understanding of the soul—if the Council approves, of course."

"Well," I switched off the heat, "the Council did allow us to obtain the salts, at least." Oasis submerged the flask in an ice bath. "We ordered them from Dell' Armonia. Runeburgh would never allow the trade of Nafs on its territory."

"We could use Egoveritas instead."

"From the black market? I don't think so," she said. She poured 11 centiliters of the cooled solution into a cup. "You saw what Egoveritas did to my father. I won't let that happen to you. We need to demonstrate a safe form of Shifting to the Council, don't we?" She offered me the cup, but hesitated. "Are you sure about this?" Worry creased her features. Naturally, no one was eager to take part in this study, so I decided to test our revised formula on myself.

"Absolutely," I said. "You're Dr. Jekyll and Mr. Utterson's daughter. If I die—"

"Don't say that, Elliot."

"If you die while trying this," I continued,

ignoring the anxiety in her eyes, "I'll be helpless attempting to run this institute alone." That elicited a smile from her, easing some tension from her brow. "Besides, I owe John and Henry for taking care of me. Without them, I would have starved or frozen to death."

She gripped the cup with her gloved hands. I reached for the tincture. "Let me do this," I said. "For John and Henry. For us, for our institute."

She looked at me and took a deep breath. "All right, but you must tell me immediately if you feel anything go wrong. Anything at all. You remember how my father's symptoms progressed?"

I remembered all too well. His symptoms began sporadically and infrequently before intensifying. His only respite was sleep and Dr. Amy's stabilizing brew.

I brought the solution to my lips. "I promise, I will. Cheers." I upended the flask and drank. I savored the taste on my tongue and waited. All I could hear was the hum of the vent hoods behind us and Oasis' anxious breathing.

"Salty," I swallowed. "Bitter taste. Stings the tongue. Warm in the gullet." We both looked at each other, then my eyes wandered, unfocused, waiting for something to manifest within me. "Ah, there we go." I bent over slightly.

"What? What is it?" She placed a hand on my shoulder.

"Heat spreading through my veins. A mild sense of euphoria," I said. "Lightheadedness." I thought I'd lighten the mood a bit. I exaggerated a clutch at my abdomen and staggered behind Oasis to the sinks, feigning nausea.

"Oh no, what have I done?!" I yelled, pretending to be in agony.

Oasis saw right through it. "Elliot, stop that." She jotted down notes in a journal. My fake yelling turned into laughter as I pushed myself away from the sink. She finished writing notes and punched my shoulder, a small smile appearing at the corner of her mouth.

"All right, all right." I took off the lab gloves and washed my hands. "We've done a lot of work today. We should rest."

We both cleaned the bench and headed upstairs. At the last step, she turned to me. "How do you feel?"

"Great," I smiled.

"Great," she replied. I didn't miss the glimmer of anticipation in her eyes.

Insight

In March, seven months before the Ceremony, I continued taking the formula: 11 centiliters, three times a day. The transient euphoria grew more pronounced each day for three weeks, accompanied by a warm tug in my chest. According to Oasis' theory, this tug was my soul responding to the formula.

I soon perceived more desires, paying greater attention to sounds. My voice was an alto, reminiscent of the soft scratch of a pen against paper, while Oasis' voice was like the gentle clink of Erlenmeyer flasks—low and harmonious.

Oasis and I returned from our teaching at the University on a Wednesday, and after a brief meal, we resumed our work on the formula. We were making progress, slowly but surely. Ten minutes after taking the dose, the warm tug returned. We left the lab together, and an unrelenting urge to listen to jazz suddenly struck me. I tapped my lap, hopping my way upstairs. Oasis laughed as she tried to catch up. "Someone's happy."

I turned to face her at the top of the stairs. "My soul's happy. Where's the radio?" I dashed to our guest room.

"Elliot, wait!" she called, her voice echoing as she hurried after me. "I have to record the changes you're feeling after this dose."

She entered the guest room just as I had cleared away the chairs and turned on the radio. Jazz was playing. Salvation.

"We'll be ready for the Ceremony soon," I said.

"Let's take it slow, Elliot." She approached me with a small grin as I danced to the melody. "We don't know where any of this is going."

"Come on, Oasis! Let's celebrate a little." I grabbed her hands and pulled her onto our makeshift dancefloor. "We deserve to celebrate."

She smiled with her eyes, but I could see tension in her every feature. I gave her hand a small tug, and she set her journal down, took off her shoes, and joined me. I felt raw and new, as if I were blooming. For the first time in eight long years, I held hopes for our institute of Lysology. And without a doubt, Oasis had her hopes as well. It felt like the sun was coursing through my veins and nerves. The fierce joy crescendoed in my head, and though I felt dizzy, I continued moving. My feet moved quickly, my focus remained impeccable. I had never experienced anything like this in my life.

Oasis and I held hands as we danced, our laughter filling the room. We moved and turned, and I caught sight of my reflection in the mirror above the fireplace next to the radio. The image in the mirror grinned. Then, with a wink, the Elliot in the mirror said, "Hey there, pretty boy!"

I screamed and stumbled back, pulling Oasis with me. She caught her footing and scrambled to my side.

"Did you see that?" I fumbled for my

glasses on the ground. Putting them on, I glanced at the clock. "Thirty minutes. Thirty minutes after my third dose," I told Oasis. She was already scribbling notes. Elliot in the mirror stood with his hands clasped behind his back. "My body felt warm, but it dissipated moments before he appeared." I pointed to the mirror. My reflection didn't point back; he just looked at me as if I were an idiot while I clambered to my feet.

"*He* has a name," Elliot said in the mirror, smiling. "The name's Fitz."

"Fitz?" Oasis glanced at me, nervousness in her eyes.

"Yeah, that was my name, right, Elliot?" Fitz said, his voice icy, his gaze fiery. That name struck a chord in me I thought I had long buried and left dry enough to disappear. But that chord wasn't completely dry. It resonated again when I looked at my reflection, it turned every sensation in my body taut, suffocating, and cold. Before Runeburgh, before Dr. Jekyll and Mr. Utterson, before Oasis, before my education and present life, there was that name. Fitz Garrison, son of Friga and Cedric Garrison. I had long buried that impoverished, downtrodden, miserable name. When I arrived in Runeburgh and met the good doctor and his husband, my name became Elliot Warlow. Only Oasis knew that part of me. But what she knew was a fragment of what Fitz in the mirror knew and lived.

Tears welled up in my chest, but instead, I chuckled. I turned to Oasis. "So the formula worked."

"Damn right it's working," Fitz clapped once.

She covered her mouth. "This is Shifting. You

Shifted!"

I turned to face Fitz. In that moment, I caught another fragment of him—of myself in the mirror that I had also long buried. Innocence.

"Your eye color's red," I said. Oasis came close to the mirror and looked at him, then at me. My eyes were a halogen green. Fitz's were a metallic red.

I saw Oasis's reflection in the mirror, a triumphant smile across her cheeks. Her reflection next to Fitz felt strange, so very strange. Oasis knew Elliot and knew little about Fitz. I had intended for no one to know about Fitz. For so long, I even hid him from myself. Yet here he was, standing next to Oasis, facing me. The image of a young man who once had dreams, love, fight, and loss, all grown up into a chemical psychologist.

Her voice brought me back to the present moment. "Perhaps this is a manifestation of your soul."

"My soul is red?" I asked, stupidly.

She snickered. "Why would the formula do that?"

"Beats the hell outta me," Fitz said. "But you made it! I Shifted."

"So we might gain the Council members' interest in the Ceremony after all," I said. I tried to explain what the Ceremony and this entire ordeal were all about, but Fitz interrupted. "I know all that." He waved me off. "I know you're revisiting Henry's formula. I know you're attending the Ceremony to bring this institute independence and continue your work with Lysology." He nodded to us with a small, somber smile. "I know everything." Something about his words pained me. *I know everything.* The words lingered in my mind for far too long. He knew everything. Everything from my dad to the factories, from the drinking to my early passions, and their destruction. Everything from why I escaped home to my acquaintance with Dr. Jekyll and Mr. Utterson, to my brewing love for Oasis that simmered three years ago and slowly bubbled.

Everything, including my insecurities, dreads, and dreams.

And it scared me.

But I didn't have the guts or strength to admit that.

Oasis sank down on the couch next to the fireplace. She whistled. "What a relief. Tell me about what you see. What you feel. We want to know everything."

"Well," Fitz dropped both arms to his thighs. "I can see the room and you." He pointed. He turned his gaze to the portrait above the fireplace, not to his right, but to the outside of the mirror, where Oasis and I stood. "I can see Henry and John's portrait." He smiled as he looked at them. He blinked the same way I do when I look at them—a blink of reverence and longing.

"I can see the same room around me, but inverted." He gazed around. "But it feels like the room exists and doesn't." Fitz put his hands in his pockets and bobbed his head left and right. "My peripheries are a little dark, hazy. I'm not even sure there's anything beyond the room that Elliot's in. I can see, hear, smell, taste, feel everything that Elliot can." He inclined his head toward me.

It was so strange to see myself in the mirror acting independently. To look at myself in the eyes and have both of us doing something completely different. One smiling, the other frowning. One's hands in his pockets, the other's hands clasped together. I sat down next to Oasis.

"Are you all right?" Oasis leaned toward me.

"Yes, I'm fine," I said. "Just—taking it all in."

"Well," Fitz said. "As long as there's no vomiting, fever, delirium, and no movement between either realm of the mirror, the Ceremony will go great."

Oasis and I frowned at him, shock in my eyes, concealed terror in hers. Now, that struck a chord in Oasis. Dr. Jekyll's last days were punctuated with those very symptoms. When he lay on his deathbed, he warned us never to let go of our passions but pursue them with great caution. He died at peace, knowing that we could learn from his example. Mr. Utterson died shortly after him, after he left the institute in our names.

Oasis shifted in her seat. "We will make sure that doesn't happen." A pause. "To either of you."

It was 10:37 pm. I was tired. We tidied the guest room and conversed with the other Elliot—*Fitz*. I saw him in every reflection and mirror, his presence giving me both peace and turmoil.

By 11 pm, Fitz's reflection dissipated, and my own returned. We decided to retire to our rooms. We had been living together in the institute, which had living amenities, as well as a library and a lab, for three years. Staying back home where Uncle John and Henry had passed away would have brought us much trouble. I ran my hand along the railing up to my room, remembering the memories, smiles, and joy we all experienced when Uncle Henry and John bought and repurposed this place.

"Elliot, a moment." Oasis put a hand on my shoulder as I approached my room. I turned to her, and she drew in a deep breath.

"What a discovery, huh?" I broke the chilling silence.

"Yeah." She kept her hand on my shoulder and gave it a little squeeze. We were both shaken by this experience. "We have to make sure you're safe, all right?" Oasis said. "This Ceremony could mean our institute's independence. But I won't risk your life for this institute. I'm not like Father."

"I know."

"You must tell me everything that you experience with Nafs. We must monitor your symptoms."

We both knew what she meant. The symptoms could sway either direction. And we knew from experience which way Jekyll's symptoms had careened.

"Since we're using Nafs instead of Egoveritas, this shouldn't result in anything undesirable, but you never know," Oasis said. A quiet moment. We looked at each other. We both knew the perils of this endeavor. "Get some rest. We've got a lot of work tomorrow." Oasis's hand left my shoulder.

We both shifted, as if something was unfinished between us. In a moment, she embraced me. I returned her embrace and allowed myself to forget everything that my apparition in the mirror reminded me of, even if only for a fleeting moment.

We disconnected and held each other's gaze for a moment.

"Goodnight, Elliot."

"Goodnight, Oasis."

Control

In the weeks leading up to April, Oasis worked tirelessly to ensure the formula was flawless in every aspect.

The formula had to begin as an off-emerald green. Upon adding exactly 0.5 grams of Nafs salts, bubbles would form, and the color would transition to a dull purple, then a crimson red. Not blood red, not orange red, but crimson. She never allowed me to pour the 11 centiliters; she was always the one to do so. Precisely 11 centiliters.

I resisted Fitz's appearance in the mirror, albeit subconsciously. I didn't want to see him. He reminded me of what I wished to forget.

By mid-April, we increased the formula's dosage incrementally. With each increased dose, the results were consistent. I would drink the formula, and half an hour later, *Fitz* would appear, remaining for thirty minutes to an hour before vanishing from the mirror.

It was a Friday, and I was in our guest room. Sitting in front of the crackling fireplace, I gazed at the portrait once more. If only Uncle John and Henry could see us now. I sat in silence, feeling their painted eyes on me as I absentmindedly rubbed my index finger. The lingering tingling sensation from the last dose should have subsided an hour ago. I glanced at the mirror and saw Oasis peeking into the guest room.

"You caught me," she admitted, sitting down beside me. "Up late thinking again?" I glanced at the clock. It was 12:28 am, and I hadn't realized the time had passed so quickly. Stirring in my seat, I blurted out, "I want more control. I want to control when he appears and disappears from the mirror."

She looked at the fireplace, mulling over the word "control" as if it were a secret. "Why?"

"He appears on his own schedule after the formula. I need control for the Ceremony." I lied; I didn't want control for the Ceremony's sake. I wanted control for my own sanity. I ran a hand through my hair, feeling the dull, prickly sensation. "I need to prove our worth for independence and funding. I want something more potent than Naf—"

"We still have seven months," Oasis interrupted, leaning toward me. I was drawn to her, lifting my gaze to meet her eyes, which held the weight of the very memories that haunted my thoughts.

Jekyll had consumed an enormous amount of Egoveritas over his year. He had calculated it once: by the end of the year, he had consumed 3,872 centiliters. A mere 1,000 centiliters was enough to induce delirium and unwanted Shifting. Even after twenty years without the salts, having left London with Utterson, the effects haunted him. Jekyll's relentless Shifting between the mirror realms had depleted his mind, body, and perhaps even his soul.

Yet the control that Egoveritas granted him over Edward Hyde was alluring. Ultimately, he lost control, but that didn't concern me, not then. I craved control and rationalized my haste because of it. *We'll figure it out. We'll make it work. We'll create a better formula.*

"Perhaps it's the reagents," I suggested. "What if it prevents me from Shifting during the Ceremony? Egoveritas would be able to—"

"Nafs is sufficient, Elliot," she insisted. "Egoveritas is unstable."

I fidgeted in my seat, yearning for control over Shifting, over Fitz. His presence reminded me of a past I had worked so hard to forget.

Oasis hesitantly placed a hand on mine, as if afraid to hold a cherished family heirloom. My hands were cold and clammy, something I didn't notice until our skin touched. "Are you still experiencing the tingling?" she asked.

"Yes."

"Elliot, listen." She guided my face to meet her eyes. "I—I'm afraid to bring this up now, but I feel compelled."

I nodded, encouraging her to continue.

"I don't know much about Fitz, and I respect your decision to keep him in the past." I tried to avert my gaze, but she cupped my jaw, and our eyes locked once more. Her next words gripped my attention. "But it seems Fitz isn't willing to remain silent. Sooner or later, he's going to reveal your—" she hesitated, searching for the right words, "—history. And I fear what that might mean for you, especially as we approach the Ceremony."

I remained silent. She swallowed. "Elliot, before I met you, before my fathers found you and took you in… you were… in a dreadful state. I'm worried that confronting your past with Fitz could—"

"I'm not fragile."

"I didn't mean it that way, Elliot."

"I'm fine. I can handle this." I pulled away from her. "I won't waste the opportunity to attend the Ceremony. It's what we've always wanted, right?"

Oasis sighed before standing up. "Come on. Let's get some sleep." She gave my shoulder a brief touch, and I stood to follow her. At the stairs, she turned to me. "Tomorrow we'll increase the Nafs dosage. See if we can achieve the control you seek."

"Great," I said. I smiled, and as she returned my smile, the tingling in my fingers intensified.

"Great," she echoed.

Confrontation

I stole a glance at the long mirror near my bed, but I couldn't hold my gaze for more than a second. He followed me through every reflective surface. I had taken my last dose of the day an hour ago, and he still wouldn't leave the mirror.

I hated seeing him, and I hated hearing his name.

He reminded me of my life before becoming Elliot Warlow, before meeting Henry and John, before Oasis, and before my education and new life.

I used to keep journals, countless journals precariously stacked near my bed. I was a passionate creator, a visionary. Fitz reminded me of that younger version of myself, of the debt I owed him.

But there was no room for visionaries in the slums of London.

Only room for factories and survival.

And drinking. A lot of drinking.

As these thoughts raced through my mind, I slammed my hand against my desk. I could sense Fitz flinching at the muffled rumble in the mirror realm where he resided. "Can you— please stop," I said, my voice shaking.

"Stop what?" he replied.

"Stop replaying those… memories in my head." My hands trembled near my face. "Say my name."

"What?" I muttered.

"Say my name. Your name."

"Your name is Fitz Garrison. My name is Elliot Warlow," I hissed.

"That's not what your mother called you."

I whirled to face the mirror, anger flashing across my face. But before I could continue, he spoke again. "He's playing a game."

My hands shook, my voice trembled. They were cold. So very cold. I could feel his breath, the raw emotion in staccato bursts. "Who?"

"Anthony," he said. "You know it."

I didn't want to admit it, but I knew.

Gale Carew, Anthony's father, was a prominent member of the Runeburgh Council of Science and Development. The Carew family, the same ones who drove Uncle John and Henry out of London, controlled what could and couldn't pass through the Council's approval. They filtered development through their whims.

Gale Carew halted Jekyll's research in Runeburgh.

Without research, there was no knowledge.

Without knowledge, no control.

Without control, no way Jekyll could survive Shifting.

I often blamed the Carews for Henry's death. If he had studied Egoveritas or Nafs, we would have been ten years ahead in our research. We might have even prevented Henry's death. The only thing he had in his final days was a hastily concocted antidote from Dr. Amy, shipped all the way from London to Runeburgh.

So when Anthony appeared on our institute's doorstep five years after John and Henry's death, inviting us to the Ceremony, it smelled of deception.

"You think he'll get off your back after the Ceremony?" Fitz's voice snapped in my mind as he paced the room. "Oh no, that's only the beginning. He'll use you, drain the life out of this institute, all under the guise of the esteemed Anthony Carew, benefactor of Lysology."

I continued to pretend the mirror wasn't in the room, but Fitz was introducing a disturbing thread of thought. With Anthony now part of the Council, after his father's resignation, our institute would become his puppet if we succeeded at the Ceremony. Soon enough, Lysology would be under the control of the Carews.

My voice caught in my throat, my breathing ragged. At that moment, I refused to believe such a possibility could be true.

"Hello? Elliot?!" Fitz tapped the inside of the mirror. I grimaced, my hand flying to my right ear as I heard the hammering in my head, synchronized with Fitz's banging against the glass.

My lips quivered with suppressed emotion. "I can't suggest anything right now. He'll—he'll withdraw our invitation."

"You're a coward," Fitz had the audacity to say with a smug smile.

I swallowed the lump in my throat. "What?" I

croaked.

"Coward," he whispered, stretching the word and savoring each syllable.

Those words. My mother and father used to call me that. Every night, after every bottle, she would call me a coward. Father had been in the factories for two years; each night, I was a coward. My explorations, my passions, my journals, all collapsed under that word. I had found work in a shabby newspaper factory.

I was still a coward.

"You're just going to let Anthony and his council control the institute, just like your mother controlled you after your father left."

I faced the mirror, my face burning hot with rage. "She was only trying to protect me!"

"Then ask yourself why you left home!"

The words tumbled beneath the anger in my chest. My hands flew to my head, and I covered my ears. "Quiet!" The word came out as a pathetic, vulnerable whisper. I looked Fitz in the eyes and turned the mirror away from me. I headed to bed and lay down, curling under my sheets like a child.

Nightmare I

I awoke to the sound of humming and singing downstairs. Startled, I bolted upright in my bed. I recognized that humming. I rushed downstairs. "Mother?"

The humming came from the kitchen. As I turned the corner towards our guest room, I caught a whiff of... strawberries?

Oasis hated strawberries. Unless it was...

"Dad?"

"Ahh, Fitz," Dad replied, a knife stained with strawberry preserves in his hand. "Please, come in. I thought you'd never wake up."

He wore a smile on his face. Why was he wearing a smile on his face?

"Good morning, Fitz," Mother's voice rang out from behind the fridge door. She closed it and turned to me. "Always the last one to wake up, huh?"

"What are you doing here?" I asked. "When did you...?"

"Arrive?" Mum finished my sentence.

"Oh, Fitz," Dad said, resuming his task of cutting strawberries. "We've always been here."

I blinked. "You've been living in Runeburgh this whole time? I thought—" I glanced behind me, hoping to see Oasis. When I couldn't find her, I faced my parents again. "I thought you were still in London."

"I was in London. With my brothers. Remember?"

I stared at her, fear bubbling up in my stomach, rising into my throat and chest. The last I knew, Mother was with my uncles after I—

"After you left me, dear. Apple?" She offered me the fruit.

I shook my head, disbelief consuming me. Leaving the kitchen, I called out for the stairs. "Oasis? Oasis?"

"Who are you looking for, dear?" Mum called from the kitchen.

"There's no one here. It's just you and us, Fitz," Dad's voice followed.

I ignored them. Something was terribly wrong.

"Oasis?" I approached her bedroom and knocked. "Oasis, please. Tell me this is a joke."

"Fitz, return for breakfast. Come back here this instant." Dad's voice grew angrier. I shook my head and swallowed hard. "Oasis!" No answer. Running my hands through my hair, my breath quickened. This can't be happening.

"Fitz, come back here."

I took a deep breath before heading back downstairs and stood between the guest room and the kitchen, where my parents gazed at me. Then Mum and Dad said something I never thought I'd hear. "So you're working on this *Lysology* now?" Dad looked around our institute. "How lovely." I couldn't miss the mockery in his voice.

All I could manage was to blink at him.

"Last time I saw you work with those *things*," Mother pointed towards our library and lab behind me. "I thought the police would come after us."

"That's why you threatened me." The words escaped my mouth before I could stop them. She frowned. "Threatened? Fitz, I was only trying to protect you."

"Don't call me that!"

"Don't raise your voice at us, young man!" Dad wagged a finger.

"Shut up," I yelled at him. "You don't get to call me or her that! You never spent time with us, and you threatened and beat me. You *never* get to defend us."

"I was working in the factories, Fitz. Working. Do you know what that word means?"

"Then you left us," I continued, ignoring his sarcasm. I turned to Mother. "And you couldn't stop drinking." I didn't miss the bottle of gin next to the pile of apples. "You just wouldn't stop."

"It was difficult for me, Fitz," she said, her voice making my eyes well up with tears. My throat tightened, and I couldn't speak. She continued, each word drawing more tears from my eyes. "You never cared about how hard it was for me. All you cared about were your foolish little experiments."

"It's my life's work—"

"Which could have entangled us with the police."

"But it didn't! You scared me. This is our work, mine and Oasis'." I stammered. "This is our institute."

"And then you decided to run away from home." She stepped closer to me, and I retreated. "Do you know what that did to me, Fitz?" I stumbled back again, nearly tripping on the carpet. "I couldn't live alone anymore. I had to live with my brothers after you and *he* left me." She jerked her head to Dad.

"I know." Tears stained my whispered confession.

"You're a coward," Dad spoke next.

I locked eyes with both of them. "Get out," I said.

They didn't respond; they just stared back at me.

"This is my work," I said. "This is our institute, mine and Oasis'. Get out of our institute. Get out!"

Dad set down the strawberries while Mum pulled something from her pocket. "All right," she said. "We'll leave. But not before you try this." She flicked a small vial from her pocket. The liquid shimmered red.

"What's this?" I couldn't take my eyes off it. It looked strikingly similar to our formula. "Oh, you should know what that is," Dad scoffed. "I thought you were smarter than that."

"It's the formula, dear." Mother placed it in my hand and headed to the main entrance. "Come on, Cedric, let's get out of here, per our son's request." She shot me a glance before opening the door. Dad walked beside her, giving me the same look. I closed the door, slamming it a little too loud.

"Oasis?" I called towards the stairs again. No answer. I headed up to my bedroom and shut the door. I needed silence.

I cradled the vial in my palm. It looked perfect. Too perfect. I uncapped the vial and brought it to my lips. The sting, the salty smell—I craved it. Without a second thought, I drank it down and set the vial on the nightstand.

My vision blurred. My head throbbed. I clenched my eyes shut and leaned over the nightstand. The pain swelled before dissipating. I took a breath and opened my eyes. Something was very wrong.

My room... it was—

Inverted.

I surveyed my surroundings. My bed is to the right, the window is to the left. The mirror is in front of me, the door is behind me.

I glanced at my clock. The numbers were inverted. I couldn't read the time. I reached for my mirror, foolishly attempting to jump through it.

The door in the mirror creaked.

"Ahh, Fitz." Dad re-entered my room on the other side of the mirror. I looked behind me at the door. No one. I could only see what the other side of the mirror framed. "I see you've tried it. As I expected. Chasing little, meaningless curiosities. Look where it's gotten you."

"Fitz, honey," Mum appeared next to Dad, arms crossed. "You're not cut out for this."

"You're not meant to explore, dear," Dad said. I pressed my palm to the glass like a child. "You're meant to stay in there."

"Where we can keep an eye on you," Mum

added.

"No." I shook my head, tears streaming down my cheeks.

"Ah, no 'no's', Fitz," Dad said. "We don't want you to get yourself into trouble and drag us along with you."

"But—but I want to grow." My voice trembled, vulnerable and hurt. "I want to learn more about Jekyll's—"

"No, young man," Dad interrupted. He approached the mirror. "Jekyll's nothing but trouble. Just like you." He looked me in the eye. "So if you want to, then go ahead. You won't be doing anything different than usual. Embarrass yourself. Waste your time alone." I opened my mouth to speak, but the mirror realm silenced me. I screamed, but the mirror's reflection swallowed my voice.

Then I woke up, mid-yelp, my breathing rapid, my skin damp with sweat. A nightmare. It was only a nightmare.

Focus

"Elliot!" Oasis burst through my bedroom door, rushing to my side. "Are you all right?" I turned to her, catching my breath. "Yes, I'm fine. It was just a nightmare." I swallowed, trying to quench the growing thirst in my throat.

I set my feet on the floor and reached for the water cup on my nightstand, emptying it in one gulp.

"Thirsty?" she asked, placing a hand on mine.

"Yeah." I blinked, realizing I *needed* my morning dose. The thirst was becoming unbearable. "Sorry, I'm all right. I didn't mean to scare you." I paused and looked at her, her brow furrowed with worry. "What day is it?"

"Wednesday."

"God, I have class today." I rubbed my eyes and got out of bed, heading to the lab. Oasis hesitated before following me. Still in my sleepwear, I prepared the formula: solvent, catalyst. "Elliot."

Nafs, stir, heat, bubble.

"Elliot."

Green. Purple. Red. I didn't wait for it to boil before plunging it into an ice bath. "Elliot!" Oasis held my shoulders, forcing me to look at her.

My mind fixated on the formula, its allure consuming me. With great effort, I tore my gaze away from the shimmering red liquid and faced Oasis.

"What happened?" she asked, unease in her voice, concern in her eyes.

My breath came in shallow gasps, and my thirst left me speechless.

"He saw his mother and father in a nightmare," Fitz's voice echoed from every reflective surface in our lab. I felt trapped, like prey caught in a predator's snare.

"What?" Oasis turned to the nearest reflection.

"What are you doing here?" I snapped at my nearest reflection. Each reflection crossed its arms. "I haven't even had my first dose."

Fitz raised an eyebrow before addressing Oasis. "I don't know how this thing works," he admitted, before focusing his gaze on me. "But your thirst for the formula might tell us something." His words hung in the air, sour and foreboding.

"That's enough, Fitz." I reached for the formula, but Oasis grabbed my wrist before my fingers touched the glass.

"That's 25 centiliters," she said.

"I'm thirsty." My lips quivered, my hands shaking under her grip. "Please, Oasis." She looked at me, and her grip weakened. I seized the flask and guzzled its contents in one gulp, the sting of the formula quenching my thirst.

Clumsily, I set the flask down and exhaled sharply, my head spinning. I left the lab and climbed the stairs, desperate to escape the ominous reflections.

"I need to switch to Egoveritas. It will give me more control over *him*." I pressed my cold fingertips into my palm, feeling my pulse. My head throbbed in time with my heartbeat. Oasis tensed her shoulders. "I said no! We're not using Egoveritas. It's unstable." I turned away, rubbing my temples until they were red.

"Elliot, listen to me." She cupped my face, forcing me to look at her. I hadn't realized I was panting, my breaths shallow and labored. "What happened?"

"He's showing me things. Reminding me of things I just—I *don't need this* right now before the Ceremony. I—"

The phone rang. We exchanged glances, unspoken words hanging between us before we headed upstairs.

Oasis answered the phone. "Hello?"

"Oasis!" Anthony's smug, musical voice came through the phone. "Listen, I thought I'd come pay the institute a visit. To go over the terms and officialities of the Ceremony with you. How's Friday next week sound?"

"Friday works."

"Wonderful! I'll be there at 5. How's Elliot, by the way?"

She glanced at me before answering. "Good. Are we finished?"

"Yes, yes. I'll see you Friday at 5! Say hello to Elliot for me."

She turned to me, a frown on her face and a softness in her eyes. As we stood on the stairs, her gaze met mine from slightly above. "Your thirst for the formula. Why?"

"Not the formula, Oasis. Control." I wrung my hands and looked away. "Every time I see him, I'm reminded of everything. The formula quiets that. I need something stronger."

"Elliot," she said, her voice resonating in my ears and quickening my heartbeat. She guided my face to meet her gaze. "I'm increasing the milligrams of Nafs to enhance the stability of the channel."

"Channel?"

"Yes, the channel between you, our physical realm, and the realm where your soul, Fitz, resides."

"Fitz is not my soul," I murmured.

"He is, Elliot." She placed a hand on my chin, sending a chill up my arms and shoulders. The sensation was pleasant, and I couldn't ignore the way Fitz's presence in my mind blossomed. When she spoke again, it was in a whisper. "Come on. Let's get something to eat before work."

Terms & Conditions Apply

A week went by with the increased dosage of Nafs, three times a day.

Control shifted toward Fitz's side. His presence awakened memories and emotions in me I had not noticed. Resentment. Fear. Memories of the factory. Father's absence, mother's despair. My destroyed journals. The drinking. The loneliness. More despair.

One particular memory that I had worked so hard to forget resurfaced the day before Anthony visited.

I was eleven years old. I had stopped paying attention to my desires and work. There was no room for passion in a home of strife.

But one night, I remembered it so vividly as though it was happening now. There was a half-moon in the midnight sky. I returned from the newspaper factory. I was depleted. My mother was in her room. Father was at the factories. Or so my mother and I thought. He had not come home for a week. I stared out the window at the moon, drained, exhaustion clouding my eyes. I blinked at the moon, and its beauty captivated me. I knew nothing in that moment, nothing but the enthralling light of the moon. It reminded me of something. The enchantment I felt at the light of the moon shining into my rickety room was the same enchantment I felt when immersed in my little explorations and discoveries. I felt captivated by something outside of my own will, drawn to my journals hidden under my bed. I pulled them out, glancing over my shoulder, as if I was committing a crime. I opened a journal and reread my notes.

> *Jekyll's a very interesting man. I didn't think*
> *I'd become interested in those things, but*
> *I'm finding myself very drawn to them!*

The eagerness in my words and handwriting, so innocent, turned sour, stinging the wounds that my early years had inflicted.

I read and read and read until I fell asleep.

Then I heard the floor creak. I jolted awake. I recognized those footsteps. They were my father's. He had returned.

The next few seconds were a blur.

Mother and father caught me red-handed. *Are you still reading those journals? Give me those!*

We don't want any trouble with the police, Fitz. If the police find these, the Carews will throw your father out of work.

And how can you have such things if you're working at a damn newspaper factory?! I made the mistake of resisting my father as he grabbed my journals. I lunged at his grasp, and his palm flew to my cheek. He gripped me by the shoulder and forced me to watch as he threw my journals out the window.

I couldn't do anything. I knew I would never see those journals again. I didn't speak a word after that as my father stormed out of my room, my mother following to calm him down. I collapsed onto my bed and pretended that I would never think of my journals again, fear and grief warring in my small, young heart, my cheek still stinging where my father had slapped me.

I blinked and found myself staring into Fitz's eyes in the mirror. Crimson pupils, innocence scorched away. I turned the mirror away, a habit I had developed since my first nightmare, and went to bed.

The night I remembered that memory, I lay down restless. The sweet break of dawn could not arrive soon enough. I needed to taste the formula so desperately. My thirst was insatiable.

The more I drank the formula, the more Fitz gained control. The more control he had, the more memories resurfaced. The more I thirsted for relief, the more I drank. A vicious cycle that I saw no merciful way out of.

It was Friday morning. I rushed to the lab, and Oasis prepared my dose. I pretended the thirst did not consume me, plagued by the vivid, unwanted memories.

I took my first dose. Two hours later, I yearned for my second.

Anthony would arrive at 5 pm. By 3:30, I took the second dose.

"Hello, Oasis." I heard the echo of his shoes as he entered the guest room. I pretended to be pleased to see him. No doubt Oasis was pretending, too. We had to pretend. Our institute depended on his good favors.

After some small talk and polite gestures over some tea, he discussed the terms of the Ceremony.

"We have several investors and exhibitionists coming to this ceremony," he said. "How did you convince them?" Oasis asked.

"I have my ways." He leaned back and offered a charming smile. "Now, let me discuss what's in it for the institute to join the Ceremony."

He pulled an envelope with his gloved hand, his movement flawless and smooth, as he set it on the table. He flicked it with his finger and winked at us. "Open it." Oasis and I exchanged glances. She reached for it and opened it. I saw her eyes scan the papers. I leaned over and read.

"That's a lot of money." The words escaped my mouth before I could think. "And the restrictions," Oasis looked to Anthony, caution in her eyes, "most of them would be lifted."

"And," Anthony raised a finger, "you'll be able to teach Lysology at the University. And eventually, at this very institute." His jacket gleamed a metallic blue under our lights as he leaned close. His style was fresh, new. I looked at mine and felt like I was stuck in the previous century. I focused on the paper, the terms, and Anthony's self-absorbed voice. "I've made a convincing argument on your behalf with the Council. If you succeed, this will be yours."

"And if we fail?" Oasis asked.

Anthony swallowed. "I'm afraid the Council

has set strict terms for that. Should you fail, which I highly doubt you will," he said, "the Council agreed to indefinitely place the institute under my supervision."

Oasis and I exchanged wary looks.

If we succeed, we gain clearance from the Council to research and teach Lysology, and receive three years' funding from the very pockets that once banned it from Jekyll. If we fail, it would forever attach our institute to Anthony's strings.

I felt a tug from Fitz's dimension, a seething, fiery rage bubbling within me. My heart thumped in my ear. Sweat formed at the back of my neck. Confront him. You coward. I swallowed. The tug grew stronger. I drowned it with some tea. I finished the cup and poured another.

Coward.

"I don't do this with all presenters, you know," he said. "If there's anything I can help you with, please let me know." Anthony stood, and we rose with him to escort him out. He offered us dinner afterward, as a 'token of peace,' he called it. We thanked him and declined. "Of course," he said. "I understand you're busy." He smiled and left.

I hastened to escape the rooms of mirrors and reflective surfaces.

Trust

Oasis led me to the small, well-kept garden of our institute. When Uncle John purchased this estate, he and Uncle Henry revived and maintained the mini garden east of its entrance. Uncle John had always loved gardening and kept an array of flower beds by the entrance window. Oasis and I had preserved them ever since. We walked past the flowers and into a grove of pine trees and conifers that shielded our institute's entrance. Our hands brushed each other, and instinctively, my fingers intertwined with hers.

I felt an immediate rush of heat blooming across my cheek and neck. I didn't look at her, but I could sense she was smirking. Then she tightened her grip around my fingers.

"Lovely day today," she said. The end of May brought with it a breath of spring. Under the sun, warmth spread over my clothes and radiated to my skin. Birds had migrated back, filling the air with the sounds of finches and insects.

"Yeah, beautiful," I said. But something poked at my mind's peace and stole this pleasant moment away. Before I could open my mouth to speak about it, Oasis addressed it with her usual directness.

"So, what do you think of Anthony's stakes in our institute?" She looked at her boots, and I didn't miss the muscle working in her jaw as her hand tensed over mine. "I don't like it," I began. "I don't want his filthy hands on our institute." I gave her hand a reassuring squeeze, and I felt her relax a little. Good, because I was going to mention something that never failed to tense both of us up. "The Carews are the reason I—"

It was Oasis' turn to ease the tension in my hand. She gave my fingers a squeeze and looked at me. I met her gaze, and she finished what was lodged in my chest, tight on my tongue. "You feel they're the reason you couldn't safely continue your work with your journals. And had to escape home."

She didn't need an answer. She already knew it. I blamed many people for what happened to me: my parents, the Carews, myself. I shifted the focus of attention away from myself.

"Yes. But shouldn't we be rightly bitter?" I had been following Oasis' steps, and she led us to a stand of pine trees. The scent of pine intensified as we stood huddled together, surrounded by the protection of the evergreens. I hated to sour this sweet moment with my words. "They were the ones who placed restrictions on Uncle Henry's research. If they didn't... he would have... he would have lived."

She shook her head. "No amount of research could have saved Father. His condition had progressed too far, and the formula he used was rudimentary, at best." A pause, and I nodded. She continued, "But perhaps we can do something about that. This is our only chance."

We moved closer, our bodies pressed slightly. Her hand went to my cheek. "Can you trust me, Elliot?"

"You're the only person I have trusted in my life."

She smiled and gave my cheek a gentle rub. I surrendered to the moment and closed my eyes. A moment of bliss passed over me. And perhaps over Fitz as well.

"Do you trust me to continue with Nafs?"

"Yes," I said without hesitation. "Yes."

"Great," she whispered.

"Great," I smiled. She brought us closer to the trees, hiding us from the world. "Why are we hiding?" My voice was hushed, quiet enough only for Oasis to hear, and Oasis alone.

"I don't know." And she kissed me.

We lingered in the kiss, feeling as though we were whole, or perhaps two pieces of something larger. We kept our foreheads close for some time after we broke our kiss, eyes closed, ears attuned to the wind, leaves, and birds. We opened our eyes. I met her gaze, and something ached inside me, somewhere unknown and unreachable. A sweet and tender ache. "We should head back. Lots of work to do," she said.

"Yeah," I smiled. I placed a hand on her temple and brushed a strand of hair before we started moving together, returning to the institute.

The daily mail arrived. A rolled-up newspaper sat at our doorstep, and I grabbed it while Oasis went for the mail. I opened the newspaper and scoffed.

Lysology Making a Comeback!
Have they changed? Tune in to Runeburgh's
Ceremony of Science and Development to find out what
the Lysologists Oasis Utterson and Elliot Warlow have
in mind for Runeburgh's scientific advancement.
October 18th, 1928
Reception 7 P.M
Ceremony starts 8 P.M.
Glass Plaza
151886 Silver Street
Runeburgh, U.K.
(turn right next to the train station, follow signs)
Get tickets today. Call:

I rolled the newspaper up and tossed it in the garbage. I turned to Oasis. She hunched over the mail, her shoulders tense, her hand covering her mouth as her eyes scanned the paper. I saw a glint in her eyes. She sniffed. Was she crying?

"Oasis?" I approached her. She turned to me. It couldn't be mistaken. Yes. Those were tears in her eyes. "Are you all right? Are you crying?"

"No, no," she sniffed. She wiped the tears from her eyes, and I did not miss the way she hid the mail away from me when I came close. "Let's head inside, shall we?" A smile returned to her face. "It's getting a little chilly."

It wasn't chilly. In fact, it was a bit warmer. But I decided not to press her. I walked alongside her, giving her space.

She swallowed as she headed upstairs to her room. "Hey, Elliot, you go ahead. I'll be right there to join you in the lab downstairs." She smiled. I knew she forced the smile, but I didn't press her. I trusted her.

"Of course," I returned her smile and headed down to our lab.

Nightmare II

*C*oward.

I tried to concentrate on the sound of running water. Yet, the various pitches and harmonies of the water and steam failed to drown out his incessant chatter. I finished my shower and gazed at the bathroom mirror. Water droplets gathered on the steam-covered surface. Wiping the glass, I revealed my green eyes. Good.

"So, you're just going to let Anthony take control of our institute that easy, huh?" I heard his voice in the mirror. I have taken my last dose an hour ago, my senses felt dulled, and my thirst was overpowering. Denying my craving for the morning dose, I turned away from the mirror and got dressed.

"This is our opportunity," I retorted. "If you don't like it, you can stop showing up. That way, we'll definitely lose the Council's favor and forfeit the entire institute to that bastard, Anthony." I didn't expect a response, but who was I kidding? I knew Fitz always had a clever comeback.

I glanced at the mirror, waiting for his sharp words and fiery gaze. "Something's wrong. He's hiding something," he said, staring at me in the mirror. "*You* can feel it too. Don't deny it," he added as I averted my eyes. I heard him chuckle. "You know Anthony's keeping secrets, don't you?"

I couldn't deny it. There was something off about Anthony, an unsettling sensation that intensified my thirst. Swallowing down the feeling, I tried to ignore Fitz, the thirst, the craving, and the bite of intuition in my chest.

I covered the mirror, turned to my nightstand, and drank a glass of water. Still thirsty. I examined my reflection in the full-length mirror. Dawn-red hair, freckles, and a lean frame. I dried my hair.

I flinched when the inside of the mirror seemed to pound, and for a moment, I thought I saw the eyes in the mirror flash red.

Thirst overwhelmed me, and my head pounded as if someone was screaming inside. I fumbled for my glasses on the nightstand. My hand shook as I reached for them, stumbling as I stepped. I collapsed onto the carpet, searching for my glasses.

"Damn it." My head throbbed in pain. Feeling around on the floor, I found my glasses and put them on. I faced the mirror, and my reflection stared back at me. I recoiled at the sight of the red irises. When my eyes readjusted, they were green again. Agony twisted within my skull, and I couldn't help but groan. I couldn't bear the thirst any longer. I lumbered down to the lab, careful not to wake Oasis.

I knew what to do. A small extra dose wouldn't hurt. Besides, I reasoned, it might even speed up our progress. I concocted any and every excuse as I prepared the additional dose, desperate to avoid facing my nagging intuition.

I drank it, the bitter liquid washing away my thirst and leaving a salty taste in my mouth. Relief washed over me. I exhaled and returned to my room.

Lying down, I closed my eyes, the relief dissolving into shame. It settled in my stomach, sour and constricting. Opening my eyes, I glanced at the clock.

The numbers were inverted.

I snapped my head back to survey the room. Everything was reversed.

I stumbled out of bed, the only light coming from the mirror before me. My bed was on my right, my bathroom in front of me. I was trapped within the mirror. I rushed towards it, pressing my hands against the glass.

"No," I protested. "No! Let me out. Fitz!"

He was on the floor, gasping for breath, on his knees. Unsteadily, he raced to the mirror. We faced each other. A sinister smile crept across his face. His red, wild, sleepless eyes met mine. He placed his hands on the mirror, his damp palms leaving imprints on the surface. Heat and steam lingered on the other side of the glass. He gripped the mirror's edges tightly, emitting a strained chuckle.

I shook my head and pounded the inside of the glass. My voice failed to break through.

Elliot?

Elliot, are you all right?

Her door creaked open.

Elliot?

He found her at my bedroom door, rushing to her and grasping her arms.

"Listen, Oasis," he implored. His voice swept through the realm in which I stood. I tried to pinpoint its source, but it seemed to be everywhere and nowhere at once. I turned back to the light from the mirror.

"You haven't slept yet? I was almost asleep when I heard something—"

She fell silent upon seeing his red irises. I hammered the mirror. He dismissed my actions with a shake of his head. Oasis frowned. "Fitz?"

"I don't have much time," he swallowed and held her shoulders. "Elliot's been taking extra doses. I keep trying to break through, but I feel more tethered to the mirror realm." Suddenly, his eyes widened with panic. He rummaged through my desk, scattering drawings and papers. "It has to be here somewhere. Where is it?!"

"What are you doing?" Oasis approached him.

A pained smile crossed his face. "Here!" He handed her a pouch. She peeked inside, blinking in disbelief.

I tried to speak, but the mirror realm silenced me. I had never touched Egoveritas in my life. *How did it get there?*

Something's wrong.

"Egoveritas…" she looked at him. "You've been drinking Egoveritas?"

"Not me! Him," he motioned toward the mirror. He approached her again, his hands trembling. "Listen.

I don't have much time." She turned to face the mirror, but Fitz redirected her gaze to his eyes.

"I don't understand…"

He clenched her arms firmly. "Please, I beg you. You have to stop them both. The realm is collapsing, and I may never escape. And Anthony. His deal will ruin everything—"

"Sleep," she commanded sternly. "Both of you. We start reducing your doses tomorrow." She broke free from Fitz's grip and headed for the door.

"No!" He lunged toward her. She was halfway to the door when I regained partial control of my body.

"We can't go to the Ceremony like this. It would be suicide for the institute," she reasoned and continued toward the door. The distance felt like miles. "I'm sure we can attend the Ceremony next year."

"But I won't be here next year!" he exclaimed.

She stopped at the door and turned.

"I don't know if I'll be able to come back," he confessed. "Not if he continues like this."

"Of course you will—"

"No." He sighed. "Damn it." He held and shook his head, anguish etched across his face. "Elliot, sit down—"

"I'm not Elliot!" he yelled, gripping his head tighter. She looked at the mirror, but I don't think she saw me. She must have seen the room's reflection and the trembling Fitz. "Please, Oasis," he whimpered. "I don't want to go."

Oasis, my closest friend since childhood, my soulmate for eleven years, and the person I loved so dearly, placed a hand on my doppelgänger's cheek. It was the most vivid and tender sensation he had ever experienced, and I felt it through the mirror realm. His hair was damp, shoulders cool, cheeks warm, and chest chirped with love and heartache.

I felt the mirror realm shudder. Beautiful, agonizing, and full of life. He wished for the moment to last forever. They shared a kiss that began with him and ended with me. I opened my eyes and met hers. She saw my green irises. "Elliot?"

Elliot.

Elliot.

I jolted awake at Oasis' voice outside my room. "Come on, we're going to be late for work."

I breathed a rushed sigh of relief. It was just another nightmare.

It was Thursday. We both had classes today. "Come on, we need to get your first dose before we head to the university."

"I'll be right there!" I sprang out of bed and got ready, anticipation bubbling in my chest at the mere mention of my morning dose.

I met Oasis downstairs in the kitchen, where we shared a quick meal before I had my first dose. We enjoyed tender moments together, a peaceful walk to the train station, and taught our classes. Back at the institute, I took my second dose, then focused on paperwork and grading before my third dose. We shared more tender moments, revisited harrowing memories, and I occasionally snuck an extra dose to quench my unrelenting thirst.

This pattern continued for three weeks, with Fitz's control over my nightmares growing ever more oppressive. Each time, I washed them away with a secret, additional dose.

The Letter

June. Five months before the Ceremony.

It had been a long day at work, and even longer in our lab. I downed my third dose, avoiding Oasis' gaze. Between work, the nightmares, and hiding the secret dose for weeks, I felt exhausted. Setting my lab coat on the bench, I let out a shallow breath.

Oasis always knew when I felt exhausted. "Come on," she said. "Meet me in the guest room. You make the tea. I'll get dad's compass."

I turned to her, amusement dancing in my eyes. "Henry's compass? That old thing? You kept it?"

She nodded. "Of course." She turned to me at the stairs. "And his scarf too."

"Don't tell me you kept the coin as well." I followed her up the stairs and smiled when she nodded.

I filled the kettle for four cups. Oasis always liked to drink two, and I often only drank one. But I made a little extra. I needed it to quench my thirst before I snuck in my extra dose in the night.

She returned with the compass and coin. I hadn't seen them in years. "I've always kept them on top of dad's things." She sat across from me.

I cleared an area on the table and turned away with my teacup as she placed the coin under the folds of Henry's scarf. This was a silly game we made up as children. We would fold Henry's scarf, which was rather large, four times, and hide the coin under it. And that compass. Oh, it was old and barely functional. Which made it perfect for the games Oasis and I used to play as children. *Find The Coin* we called it.

I looked to the portrait to my left. "We could very well lose this whole institute if I mess this up."

"No peeking!" Oasis said. I turned my back again and laughed. "We won't lose the institute, Elliot."

"Can I turn around now?"

"Yes. First move?"

I took my first move over the grid-like pattern of the scarf. I moved in one L shape and tracked the compass' needle. It barely moved. With a smile, she gestured for me to turn around again, and I did as she shuffled the coin under the scarf once more. My fingers tingled. I looked at my palms. If anything were to happen to me, I needed her to know. "You're brave, you know, Oasis," I said.

"You can make your next move now." She took a sip of tea and smirked. "Tell me more."

"I don't think I would have been able to do this without you."

She put down her tea. She took a deep breath and looked at the fire. "That's not entirely true."

I took another move. The needle quivered. I was getting closer. I smiled and raised an eyebrow. "I get another move."

She smiled. Our eyes met.

"So that means I'm close?"

"I didn't laugh. It was a simple smile. Take your move," she said.

I moved it in another upside-down L shape. Oasis snickered.

"So I am close!" I said.

"Maybe," she said. Her smile dissolved, and she leaned over the scarf, close to me. "Your eyes are tired."

I moved the compass again, and the needle moved lazily right. I pulled the coin out and placed it in her palm. "Found it," I said.

Oasis set the coin and our cups of tea aside and took a breath. "You look like you haven't slept in a week," she said. "What are you hiding?"

I averted my gaze and drew in a breath. "Nothing." The word left my tongue, barely audible.

"I laugh when you're close to the coin. But you," Oasis said, "you avert your gaze." I faced her again. The task felt insurmountable. But I leaned closer to her, drawn by a force too great for me to control. "So this game was a trap," I said, my voice tinged with both amusement and worry.

"Something like that." She cupped my cheeks and embraced me. "What are you hiding?" she whispered. Her whisper sent a tingle in my ear as I closed my eyes, our bodies pressed together.

"Nothing," I said. "The formula's working just fine. The Council cannot refuse our data." She planted gentle kisses on my temple, then moved down my neck. "True. But you're a terrible liar," she whispered, her lips brushing past my ear.

I chuckled. "You want to do this here?" I broke away from her, every muscle in my body yearning to return to her embrace. "Or..."

"My room," she finished. She stood and traced a finger along my lower lip. I followed her.

She patted the bed. I wasted no time in holding her in my arms, the pressure of our bodies together igniting a fire within me. She kissed me, her hands meeting at the nape of my neck. "What are you going to wear to the Ceremony?" she said between kisses, her lips moving gracefully as though my neck was her dance floor.

"A bowtie." I tilted my head, exposing my neck to her, a breath of joy escaping my throat as her lips trailed down my shoulder. "You?"

She pulled back, a coy grin on her face. "You'll just have to wait and see." I returned her grin and pressed her against me, wrapping her arms around my waist, our breaths syncing with bubbling desire. I led us down to her pillow, sharing tender, innocent love, our hands exploring each other's bodies with gentle caresses. Her arms wrapped around my back, and mine cradled her cheeks. We shared a passionate kiss.

I should have kept my eyes closed. I should have surrendered to that moment and allowed love and trust to unite us.

But I spotted something in the corner of my eye that would shake our trust. An open letter. With *Fitz's* name on it.

I stopped. Oasis frowned. "Are you all right?"

She intertwined her hands behind my neck.

I pulled away and reached for the letter. "I didn't know I received mail..."

"Elliot, wait—" She tried to take it away, but it was already in my hands. I frowned at the date. *May 17th, 1926.* That was over a month ago. I stood from the bed and opened the letter. "Elliot, please." She lunged to grab the letter from me. But it was too late. I recognized the handwriting.

It was my Uncle Harrison's.

I read the letter aloud, my eyes seeing, my mouth reading, my mind disbelieving. "Dear Fitz. I hope this letter finds you well. As you know, your mother has been living with us since you left for Runeburgh. Her health has been deteriorating for years. I had to write and send this letter in haste as your mother passed away last weekend. I know how much you were against being there for your father's passing, and I do not blame your absence from his funeral. But I implore you to come to London for your mother's. It would mean so much to her... with patience and love... your uncle Harrison." My eyes welled with tears. I blinked, and they fell to my cheeks as I turned to face Oasis. Her eyes brimmed with tears as well. "Elliot, I can explain. Please."

"This was four weeks ago. The funeral was..." I glanced at the letter again, the words blurring beneath my furious tears, "the funeral was a week ago." My voice choked with emotion, and all I could do was shake my head. "Why didn't you tell me?"

"Because I was afraid it would break you." She stood and tried to hold my hands, but I stepped away from her. "We—we were doing so well. And... Anthony's terms for the institute were... too good. The funding, the support. I was afraid that you would—"

"What? Fail? Mess up the Ceremony?" I said, my voice rising with the anger that boiled in my chest and spread through my body. "Am I that fragile to you?"

"No. No, I didn't mean it that way, Elliot." She whispered, her voice barely audible. "Please. You have to understand. I meant to tell you, I swear." She attempted to reach for my hands again, but I didn't let her. "I was going to tell you. But then—I postponed it a day. Then two. And a week went by and..." Tears streamed down her cheeks. "Please, I'm... I'm so sorry."

I shook my head. I don't know what came over me, but I tore the letter apart and threw it across the floor. I turned to her, heartbreak, anger, and despair warring in my chest. "You—you lied to me. You..." My hands flew to my mouth, and I had to look away from her. I turned my back to Oasis, my voice shaky when I spoke next. "You asked me to trust you."

"Elliot, please." She placed her hands on my back and shoulder.

I shrank away. "Don't touch me!" I ran out of her room and hurried to the stairs. "Elliot, wait!" she called after me.

I turned to face her, struggling to find the strength. "For what? Hmm? So you can lie to me again? First, it was my mother. What's next?"

"I meant to tell you, I swear. I just didn't want to hurt you." She descended two steps toward me. I moved four steps away from her.

"You've already hurt me!" I opened my mouth to speak, forever regretting the words that I spoke next. "You're sick, Oasis!"

"Elliot, I'm not sick, I'm scared!" Her voice echoed through the staircase. I faced her, fresh tears welling in her eyes. "I'm scared. I don't know what will happen to you from one moment to the next with this formula. And after my father died, I had nothing left but this institute and you." She took a few cautious steps toward me, her eyes full of longing. "I just wanted you to be okay."

I felt an irresistible urge to take the formula. Fitz's voice skittered in my mind. *She's just like him. Just like Anthony. Liars.* My hands trembled as hers came to meet my cheeks. I nearly forgot that I was hiding something from her as well.

"Please, Elliot. We can fix this. I promise. Just give us a chance."

"You're right," I said. My hand met hers, and a faint smile spread across her cheeks. But that smile was short-lived. "I lied to you, too. I was hiding something." Her furrowed brows urged me to say more. "I've been taking extra doses of the formula. I needed to **purge** him. In fact." I pulled away from her. "I want a dose *right now*. Right after you leave."

"What?"

I pointed to the door. "Leave. Now, Oasis. Please. I can't stand being next to you." Silence fell, and thunder rumbled outside.

"Why did you hide this from me?" she asked, tears shimmering in her eyes like polished marble.

"I—" My breath grew heavy. "I don't know."

Absently, she walked to the closet, strapped her boots on, and headed for the door. I stood and watched her. We turned to each other, and our tearful gazes met. She opened the door. "Take care of yourself, Elliot Warlow." And she left.

The door echoed as it closed. Then I stood, engulfed in silence, humiliation, and loss. My trembling arms dropped to my sides, and I turned to face the institute, alone. I stood in the entrance hall, panting, trying to grasp what had just happened.

An overwhelming thirst consumed my thoughts, and without hesitation, I prepared a dose and drank it. Rage surged through my arms, and I flung the flask across the lab. It smashed against the door and shattered. The scale was next, then the pipette, and soon the lab bench lay in shambles.

I raced to my room. The mirror faced me, reflecting my entire image, from red hair to a half-buttoned shirt and bare feet.

"God damn it." A sob escaped me. Then a wail. "Damn it!" Breathless, I screamed and hurled the mirror to the floor. I heard it crack. I stumbled toward it and stared at my reflection. Green eyes glinted behind stale tears, my face split in the shattered glass. Then I collapsed to my knees. I clasped a hand to my mouth as if to hide my pitiful weeping from the mirror. Tears seeped through the cracks in my palm and splattered the mirror.

Rain pattered against my window. I was utterly alone.

Egoveritas

I awoke in a cold sweat, shivering, shaky breaths rattling my body.

The first thing I heard was the ticking, the relentless *hammering*, of the clock in my room. So very loud. My heart thudded inside my chest. I stumbled downstairs, swallowing hard. I recalled what had happened the previous night and remembered that I was alone. The institute was empty. The only sounds I could hear were my breath and footsteps echoing in the hall. The silence was haunting.

I headed to the kitchen. Water. I needed water. I held a cup under the sink, my hand trembling, and filled it. I downed it in one gulp.

"Damn it." I was still thirsty. I opened the fridge again.

Apple juice. Too sweet.

Orange juice. Not bitter enough. But it would have to do.

I drank it down.

Damn. I needed something salty.

Salted almonds. I grabbed a fistful from the cupboard and ate them with shaking hands. Every mouthful tantalized me with relief, satisfaction lapping away on my tongue with each bite. My breath trembled. I craved bitterness and saltiness. My damn reflection on every surface irritated me.

I was alone. Oasis couldn't tell me what to do. She couldn't tell me how worried she was about me. She wasn't here to temper my impulses. And I felt crushingly lonely. But somewhere deep inside my soul, I reveled in being alone. A small voice in my head echoed, bouncing off the vestiges of my mind and amplifying.

Runeburgh Alchemy and Apothecary Square.

Suddenly, I was in the guest room. I blinked and found myself looking at the mirror. My reflection was mine, but the eyes were not. They were Fitz's red.

Runeburgh Alchemy and Apothecary Square.

As if possessed, I headed outside the institute. I walked and walked until I reached the train station. Beyond the train station, there was the Runeburgh market.

But the Square was underground. And I knew exactly how to find it.

After all, this was how I ended up in Runeburgh after escaping London. It was there that the good doctor, Henry Jekyll, found me, alone, hungry, and cold.

I arrived at the Square. Memories flooded my mind as though the space was sentient and willed those memories into being.

I was a boy of eleven. I had crept out of my parents' house with nothing but a small duffle bag with minimal supplies, and arrived at the London train station. I remember the guilt, the shame, so acute, it felt like daggers in my young heart as I handed the money that was supposed to go to our rent, to the train out of London. I didn't care where it headed. Glasgow, Liverpool, Manchester. When I next exited the train, I arrived in Runeburgh.

The Square was the first place I arrived at after leaving the train station. I walked mindlessly and ended up there.

I begged for spare change to sate my hunger, but no one paid attention to a little lad like me. I spent three nights sleeping under an abandoned shop tent. I could barely move when Dr. Jekyll found me and brought me home to John and Oasis.

I never wondered why he, a respectable gentleman scientist like himself, was in the Square. Now I knew exactly why. Because I was about to do the same thing. The Square was exactly how I remembered it. I hadn't been there in years. I walked past vendors and shops all the way to a tent. I headed inside and entered the hidden door underneath. Good. It still opened.

I entered a room filled with swirls of fog and smoke. I was in the right place. The perfect location to hide scientific contraband right under the Council's noses.

But where to find what I needed?

My feet moved as if guided by some insatiable desire to quench my thirst. "Want some special crystals, young man?" a person said from behind a cloth-covered table. "Oh, you're not just any young man," they continued, leaning out of the shadows with a smoking pipe between their grinning lips. "You're Warlow, aren't you?" I turned to them. The mirror behind them startled me, though Fitz wasn't there. The formula must have worn off. My throat was raw. I needed it.

"Yes," I said. "Yes, I am."

"Heard about your entrance into the Ceremony. How's it going?" they blew a puff of smoke in my face. I drew in a trembling breath and rubbed my eyes. They scoffed. "So it's not going well, huh?"

"Listen," I said, opening my eyes. "I need Egoveritas. Do you still have that here?"

"Depends on how much you're willing to pay," the person said.

I reached into my pocket and pulled out what I could. "Will this do?"

"Oh, this will do just fine," they replied. They took the money and turned around, rummaging through their shelves and boxes. I held my breath.

"All the way from Dell'Armonia, this little pouch came." They placed a pouch on the table, a small cloud of purple puffing beneath it.

I exhaled as I held the pouch. "Thank you," I said. "Thank you."

The person grabbed my wrist before I could leave. "Warlow." I turned to them. "I'm rooting for you." They released my arm.

I hurried outside into the open air. I took the train back to the institute and rushed to the lab, ignoring every reflective surface.

I felt possessed as I entered the lab.

Three grams of Egoveritas, poured into 20 centiliters of solvent. Add 1 milliliter of autolysine and 4 milliliters of a catalyst. Bunsen burner. Cool it in ice. Gravity filtration. Green. Purple. Then red. 17 centiliters.

I looked at the ruby tincture. I could see the reflection of my eyes in it.

Drink it already.

"Bottoms up." I drank the flask whole.

My abdomen erupted in flames, my hands trembling. My fingers couldn't hold the flask anymore, and it slipped through my grasp. But at least my unyielding thirst was quenched. I stood upright, regaining my bearings.

I took two steps before I had to sit down again. My vision blurred. I shook my head and tried to find balance on the bench.

Nausea. A grinding in my bones. It was maddening. I stumbled onto a bench chair, nearly knocking over more flasks and the already mangled scale. My joints ached, and I had to unbutton my shirt. Pain and discomfort surged beyond my viscera. My head throbbed with a sharp, stabbing pain. I *felt* my soul, my very spirit, gagging. Bile bubbled in my stomach. I turned to the sink.

"Oh, God."

I hung my head over it, waiting for the almonds and orange juice to come out. My breathing quickened. Freezing and melting at once. I shook my head weakly. So much noise. The sink, the clicks, the lab vent, the building airways. Too much noise in my head. Too much noise in my chest. Too much. I shut my eyes. I waited and held tight.

At last, the nausea subsided. The pain diminished. My head still spun, but the stabbing sensation was gone. The joint pain lessened. I lifted myself and opened my eyes slowly, wincing at the brightness. I stumbled to the lab lights and switched a few off. At least I wasn't thirsty anymore.

I glanced at the reflective surfaces of the cabinets. It was still Elliot, but I felt Fitz within me, somewhere behind the mirror, just beyond the threshold between his realm and mine. With one eye closed and the other half-opened, I nodded. A few more doses, and I think I'll have full control.

I placed my hand on my belly and shuffled forward before stepping on something that crunched.

The broken flask. "Oh, fuck."

I hastened to clean the shattered glass. Slowly but surely, the job was finished. I tidied the lab bench as if I hadn't thrown it into disarray the other night. I headed upstairs, showered, and changed my clothes. I drank some water, brushed my teeth. The clock ticked, but there was no pounding in my head, no raging thirst. It was 11:07 pm. I lay down in bed, closed my eyes, and waited for sleep to come.

Nightmare III

When I opened my eyes again, it was 2:45 am.

Restless and overheated, I threw off the covers. So hot. I needed air. I descended the stairs barefoot and stepped into the cool gardens. I closed my eyes and let a nightly breeze wash the sweat on my neck.

I moved to the middle of the garden where the bushes and flowers were the thickest. I breathed the open air and gazed around me. The stark, pale flowers were more fragrant at night. I smelled them with such intensity. Nocturnal creatures were wide awake. Midnight was midday to them. My body felt slow, my reflexes heavy. My head was full of unwanted scrap, and distant, loud, inaudible chattering. I sat down at a bench, put my elbows to my knees, hands clasped, and hung my head. I let the weight within my mind sit in one place for some time.

The institute was supposed to be our dream. Now, it feels like a nightmare. I felt like a puppet. A puppet for Anthony. A puppet for Fitz. Like I was for my first family. I thought I could cut those puppet strings by joining the Ceremony. I felt entangled with a thousand more strings.

But nothing felt harrowing as realizing that I was merely a puppet for Oasis as well. My chest ached. My throat went dry. The fucking thirst again. "Another dose it is then," I muttered, lifting myself up, my left hand to my knee.

But something felt wrong.

Cold grasped my body, weighed down my limbs. I felt like I was being pulled back into a reflective surface.

I rushed forward. I needed to purge him with Egoveritas. Fast!

Nausea captured me again. I leaned on the small light pole, the hateful sensation blurring my vision. I staggered forward. Things were darker. The night ambiance went quiet. When my vision refocused, I was suddenly looking into my bedroom from the inside of the covered mirror.

Footsteps drew behind the glass. I could hear my breathing, amplified, echoing. Cold. So very frigid.

The cloth against the mirror took the shape of a hand, fingers, then a clenched fist. I braced myself.

Someone removed the cloth.

Her eyes reflected my own. I pressed my hands against the mirror, the glass a cruel barrier between her skin and mine. "Oasis?" I called to her, but she couldn't hear me. Elation and despair clashed within me. I hammered the inside of the phantom glass. I pounded louder and harder, the mirror realm booming back at me. In an instant, I was gripped by a paralyzing dread. Why was I afraid?

My heart hammered in my chest.

"Oasis!" I hammered again, the sound muffled and low. I found her at my desk. She opened a drawer and pulled out a vial.

I don't remember putting a vial in there.

The scene arrested my muscles and all I could do is stare as she held the vial, her brown eyes reflecting the jewel-red liquid.

She turned to the mirror.

"Yes." I smiled meagerly. "Yes, Oasis I'm here. Get me out!" I tapped the glass with my palm. She walked past me like I wasn't even there. I tapped harder and faster. "Oasis!" I screamed.

She found the pouch of Egoveritas on my nightstand. My blood ran cold.

I heard her footsteps come toward me. My heart fluttered with salvation. She recognized me. She wasn't surprised, she wasn't confused. She was… Angry, disappointed, resentful. I could only shake my head. She frowned, her teeth gnashing. Tears welled in her eyes, and she threw the vial and pouch of the cursed salts to the mirror. Glass met glass, and the realm where I was echoed with a wild, resounding rumble. My head rang. Oasis stormed out of my room.

"No! Don't leave."

But you're the one who asked her to leave.

A stark, white-hot pain grasped my stomach and I bent and held my abdomen. I screamed, one hand still on the glass. The pain held my body in a knot. My insides felt so tangled. I couldn't breathe.

The glass disappeared beneath my palm, and I tipped forward. The pain subsided. I opened my eyes and gasped air. I was on the carpet in my room. I barely re-orientated myself before I got to my feet and ran forward. I nearly tripped getting to the door. My feet slid across the floors and stairs.

"Wait!" I could barely catch my breath. "Wait, Oasis, please."

I found her halfway down the stairs. "Why? Huh, Elliot?" She whirled on me. "You're the one who booted me out of the institute. And for what? So you can drink Egoveritas?" Words knotted in my mouth. I felt like an idiot.

"So you can end up just like Father and die? You know I have no one but you in this world."

I reached to her, she shrunk away. I took a cautious two steps to her; she went four down. "We grew up together. We had a dream together. We built this institute together. Doesn't a slight bit of responsibility weigh down on you?" her voice cut through the silent staircase. I took a step to her and she stayed still.

"Please, Oasis I—" I stammered. I put my hands to her cheeks. "Forgive me."

"And I thought we were growing this friendship into something more."

"We were Oasis," I whimpered.

She shook her head. "You're a terrible liar Elliot. A terrible scientist and a terrible friend." My throat went dry. I blinked a couple of times at her before she broke away. "You know," she continued. "You're right for kicking me out. I never wanted to stay with you anyway." Her voice rose ice caps in my chest.

"What?"

"Because you are a failure, Elliot. No wonder." She took steps toward a coat hanger. It began to rain and thunder, the outside world a tragic orchestra, and our institute a stage.

I raced to her.

"Yeah, and you know what?" She hastily put her coat on, tears streaking her gaze. "You're really stupid. Who takes up a silly little project like that?" She grabbed an umbrella. "It's dangerous. I knew it was dangerous. But I left you do it." She grabbed her boots next. "I helped you, in fact. I helped you end yourself."

"Oasis, what do you mean?"

"You're sick, Elliot." Her words resounded in my head. Words escaped my tongue. She reached for the handle of the door and left into the rain, slamming the door behind her. The doors echoed. Time was like a dream.

I turned around. This wasn't right.

The entire entrance hall was covered in mirrors.

Rimless mirrors, rims of brown. Rims of gold. Victorian rims, circular rims, square rims, floral rims. All framing the reflective surface. And behind each surface stood Fitz, his face contorted in a scowl.

I turned away. More Fitz. I turned to my left. Fitz. Right. Fitz. I scanned the entire room. More Fitz. His face sullen, his gaze but a husk of a soul that never was and never will be. Wait. What's this?

I stepped to the mirrors on the stairs.

"Uncle Henry?" I said like a child. I let tears cover my sight and slide down my cheeks. "Uncle

John?" I saw John next to him. They smiled. I smiled stupidly and came closer to them. They won't leave me.

Their smiles dropped and mine did as well.

"Why did you do this Elliot?" Uncle John scolded.

"Do what?" I tried to say.

"You shouldn't have done that young man," Henry said. They both shook their heads at me.

I turned away from their heavy frowns and ran past more mirrors. One mirror stopped me in my tracks. Jekyll. The reflection had green eyes. He didn't have green eyes. His eyes were dark brown.

I approached him. His face was stern, without emotion. His eyes followed me as I came closer. He towered me.

"You'll be damned to hell, *Fitz*," he grumbled.

I bolted away to the guest room and ran past Fitz and Fitz and more Fitz. My hands flew to my ears and eyes and face. It was so loud again. I covered my senses and shook my head. My feet carried me to face the fireplace.

The portrait, where did they go? In place of John and Henry, there was Anthony Carew. "I must thank you, Mr. Warlow," he grinned. My face twisted in a grimace. The portrait continued. "This institute is all mine now."

"No!" Without thinking, I grabbed whatever was within reach and wrenched it at the portrait. I stumbled out of there and dashed past the mirrors, to my room. I rested my back at the closed door and shut my eyes.

This is delirium. Some sleep would help.

But when I opened my eyes, my bed was inverted.

I was inside the mirror again, facing the glass, my breath rattling my body. Through the mirror, Fitz stood calmly, back to the door, holding a vial of red, grinning smoothly, readily.

He rocked the vial back and forth gently with his fingers. "So tell me." He pushed himself from the door. "How do you like it in there pretty boy? Enjoying the cold? The silence? Hmm?"

I could do nothing but tap the inside of the glass.

He laughed. "Coward. You're a coward Elliot. You know," he walked closer to the mirror, his head bowing to me, "I always knew there was something a little off. Something Anthony did not want you to know. His deal was too perfect." He lifted his head and gazed at me. Frigid. I felt so very frigid. "And if you won't do anything about it, then I suppose I must." He moved the vial threateningly close to his mouth.

"No!"

Fitz laughed. He waved the vial in front of his mouth and nose, saving every whiff of it. I could smell its sting in the mirror realm, and I ached for a lick of it.

"You know, as your soul," he shot me a glance, "I could sense hers as well." I saw longing in his eyes. "I could feel her soul in the mirror realm when she was around. She really cared for you. But you betrayed each other." He clicked his tongue. "Now I can't feel her presence in the mirror at all." He pulled the vial to his lips.

"No, Fitz listen!"

"Oh so now you want to talk?" he said. "I don't think so."

He knocked it down and savored every degree of sensation.

"Ah! That was good." He threw the vial to his side. It broke against my bedframe. "Now for the finale." He reached into his pockets. I saw him pull out the compass and coin. "How did you get those?" I said. "Give them back." I hammered the glass. "Mmm," he thought and pursed his lips.

"No."

Fitz walked to my bedroom window and threw it open. He waved the coin and compass in front of me and flung them out the window. I heard a splash. I ran to the window in the mirror realm and looked out.

A vast sea. The institute sat in the middle of the sea. I could see no land around. "No." I shook my head. "This can't be happening. This is a nightmare." I closed my eyes shut. I'll wake up soon.

I turned to the mirror and ran to face him. He sat at my desk and grinned.

I yelled to him and tried everything in my palms' power to leave the mirror. Strings materialized on my wrists and pulled me back. I looked behind me. There they stretched into an unknown origin in the darkness. I tried to fight them but to no avail. They tangled. Fitz laughed. I turned to face him on the right side of the mirror, but something wrapped around my mouth. I tried to look. Jekyll's scarf. I tried to fight but nothing happened.

The mirror realm filled with water. The scarf

soaked.

I bolted awake, screaming, my breath heavy. I jolted out of bed and faced the mirror. No Fitz, just Elliot. I opened my nightstand drawer through instinct.

The compass, coin, and scarf were still there, right where I left them the night after I so stupidly told Oasis to leave.

I pulled them out and hugged them close as I curled back into my bed. "I miss you." The words left my mouth on a shaky breath. I buried my face in the scarf and sobbed. "I need you…" I whispered.

I wanted her back. So very sorely.

But first, I needed to find the right ring.

The Ring

I walked two planes of existence—his and mine. Fleeting glimpses of his realm appeared as I made my way to the train station.

I rode the train and journeyed toward my destination: an antiquated jewelry shop. Heavy wood and a thick layer of dust characterized its Victorian design. This shop was the only place I knew that just might have what I wanted for the change that I had.

As I entered the shop, I scanned my surroundings. Mirrors were absent, but any gem or diamond could be a dangerous, reflective surface. Taking a deep breath, I browsed through the exquisite jewelry.

The jeweler behind the desk observed me through his magnifying lens. I strolled, clasping my hands behind my back, and pretended I didn't see scrutinizing gaze. His hair, a silvery hue, seemed to mimic the silver pieces displayed behind the glass. He was dressed in a double-breasted waistcoat, shades of dark navy blue dominated his attire, save for the off-gold trim adorning his cuffs, collar, and waistcoat. He offered me a smile when our eyes met, and I reciprocated before continuing my search from one ring to another. "Can I help you with anything, young man?" he inquired.

Startled by his voice, I replied, "I'm looking for a ring. I'm proposing to someone."

"Wonderful," he beamed, lowering his magnifier. "Congratulations." With a gloved hand, he beckoned me closer to his desk.

"I have a fine collection," he stated. "But tell me, what are you looking for?"

"I'm seeking something unusual, if that makes sense," I explained. "Something that looks like..." I paused, searching for the right expression. The sparkle of the jewels inspired me. "...like it both exists and doesn't."

His smile widened as he raised both index fingers, signaling for me to wait. "I've got just the ring." His muffled voice came from beneath the desk as he ducked under it. I listened to the sounds of rustling bags and the creaking of a box—it was refreshing to hear things without seeing them.

The elderly man emerged with a box, placing it on the table before revealing its contents. I leaned in for a closer look.

The ring was of an aged elegance, with intricate etchings that extended from the gemstone along the band's shoulders. The central stone, held in place by prongs that surrounded it in a delicate yet purposeful pattern, was of an indescribable hue. It seemed to shift between murky gray, white, and a tinge of purple. It delighted me. It delighted Fitz as well. I asked the jeweler how much it was.

He stared into my eyes for a moment before

blinking and asking, "Young man, do you know someone by the name of Utterson?"

Taken aback by his question, I responded, "My friend whom I'll be proposing to. She's his daughter. John Utterson and Henry Jekyll were her parents. They, uh..." Emotion welled up within me, and I blinked back tears. "They took good care of me."

"Ahh, I see," he acknowledged. "What a small world. John bought his ring for Henry from this very shop."

I smiled, the heaviness in my chest transforming into a bittersweet warmth. "Small world indeed," I agreed.

"For you, young man, I'll offer the ring at half its price," he declared.

"Really, sir? Are you sure?"

"Yes, of course," he assured, waving a hand in dismission. "And besides, it's been here for years, and I'd like to see it find a new home." He chuckled, and I joined in. "It's a beautiful ring," the old man remarked. He carefully placed it back in the box and tied a neat bow before handing it to me. "Good luck, young man."

"Thank you, sir," I replied. I reached into my pockets, handed him the payment, and gently nestled the ring box into my pocket.

I walked outside the shop, feeling a heaviness and lightness at once. A throbbing headache and a sweet warmth in my chest commanded my senses. I swallowed and made my way back to the train station.

Rumors

"Mr. Warlow? Mr. Warlow."

I tensed, raising my shoulders in defense. Only strangers addressed me like that—strangers who wanted to ask questions or pester me, or both. Ignoring them, I quickened my pace.

"Wait a moment, Mr. Warlow," the voice persisted. The sound of footsteps hastened to match my speed. How awkward. I turned around with a forced smile. "Yes?"

"Oh, hello," the individual stammered, appearing shy, polite, and a bit too eager. "I work with the Council. Well, not exactly—but as a journalist for the newspaper, *The Conrad*. I collaborate with them indirectly. Umm, hi, I'm Evan Kingsley."

"Hello," I replied, injecting extra politeness into my tone as I continued walking. Evan fell into step beside me.

"I recognized you and just wanted to ask you a few questions," Evan explained. "Sorry, I can't take questions right now. I need to catch a train," I said, hastening my stride.

"No, no, they'll be quick, I promise," Evan

assured, keeping up. "How is the study progressing?"

"I'm afraid we can't discuss that before the Ceremony," I deflected.

"I completely understand," Evan conceded. "I've heard the Council members are excited about this year's ceremony."

"I'm sure there will be lots of incredible exhibitions," I said.

"I've heard some rumors of bribery within the Council," Evan said.

"Do tell." My pace slowed, and I turned to face Evan.

"I wanted to gather more information, so I thought I'd approach you. I'll be attending the Ceremony to collect additional details as well."

I stopped and faced Evan squarely. "I'm afraid I haven't heard of such rumors." Anger simmered within me. "Which Council members were involved?"

"Well, I'm not sure which ones, but I learned there were three."

"When?"

Evan furrowed their brow, deep in thought. "I believe it was eight years ago." That was around the time the Council imposed restrictions on Jekyll's research. My gaze dropped to the ground. There was only one person who could have bribed three council members.

Gale Carew. Anthony's father.

"I heard some people were concerned that bribery might be an issue in this year's ceremony," Evan continued. "Is the institute of Lysology worried as well?" Thoughts raced through my mind, weaving a blurry image. Anthony's enthusiasm for Lysology's resurgence seemed odd. There had to be strings attached. Somewhere, deep within, my very soul convulsed in turmoil. *He* ached to find an answer, and I felt him pounding on the walls of my mind, clawing for control of my body. "I have to go, Evan."

"Wait, I have a few more questions!"

Clutching the box close to my chest, I sprinted toward the train station. My legs pounded in sync with the throbbing in my head. The realm where he resided began to boil and trap heat. My eyes burned, yet no tears fell. I pressed my icy hands under my eyes to soothe them. Nausea overwhelmed me. The cacophony in my head amplified, and I thought I could hear him bellowing in fury. He flooded my mind with curses and accusations. I entered the train and tried to focus on the sounds of its engine.

I disembarked and made my way to our institute, stumbling along the paved, flower-lined paths leading to the entrance. I stepped into the eerily silent institute, my mind fragmented between the oppressive mirror realm, Carew, the ceremony, the formula, and Oasis. I struggled to keep the pieces from falling apart.

Retribution

My index fingers pressed against my lips, silencing me. But the thoughts in my mind couldn't be silenced.

Find him. Make him talk.
Get the institute what it deserves.
Oasis deserves to know.
Find him and make him pay.
I warned you he was planning something. But you wouldn't listen to me.
You wouldn't even listen to yourself.
Coward.

The weight of the ring box and the pouch of salts in my pockets anchored me at the present moment. I needed sleep. I closed the door to my bathroom, covered my bedroom mirror, placed the box and pouch of salts on my nightstand, and went to bed.

But sleep eluded me. Electric anxiety gripped me, sweat dampening my sheets. I longed for the formula. I longed to *act*.

Taking a deep breath, I staggered to my drawer. Excruciating pain, a grinding in my bones, and a soul-wrenching nausea overtook me. Dizziness forced me to clutch the nightstand for balance. Breath escaped my chest as soon as it entered, my vision blurred. *Find him. Make him talk.*

I clenched my eyes shut and tried to shake the urges from my head, all echoing in Fitz Garrison's voice. But he wouldn't relent.

A grunt escaped me as I attempted to stand upright. As my vision readjusted, thirst returned. I was possessed by something, *someone* beyond my control. I snarled and grabbed the pouch of salts, lurching to the lab.

I put the formula together with a speed I could not recognize, not fully cognizant of my actions. But instead of Nafs, I used Egoveritas—a purple liquid that shimmered under the white lab lights.

Thirty centiliters. Nothing less would quench my thirst.

With a trembling hand, I raised the concoction to my lips. Fitz waited anxiously, eagerly, for me to surrender.

As the first drop touched my tongue, I downed the rest greedily, like it was my first sip of water after a long, hot day. Its bitterness stung as it coursed down my throat. I set the flask on the bench. My thirst was sated, my mind quieted. I stumbled towards the stairs, desperate for a lick of sleep.

As I reached the entrance hall, ready to ascend to my merciful bed, a searing pain tore through me. "My God," I grunted, clutching my abdomen and doubling over. Pain contorted every muscle in my face.

At last...

Fitz's voice boomed through my mind. My hands shot to my hair, attempting to claw the thundering voice out of my head. "Get out!" I warned, weakly.

The *torment* flared again, devouring me, consuming me. I collapsed to the cold stone ground, pleading, "Get out of my head!"

He responded like a caged beast, his claws tearing through me, pain reaching every corner of my body. "You're insane!" I screamed, my voice morphing into a cackle as he ripped out of me and flung me into the mirror realm with such violence that I keeled over.

Fitz drew in a sharp breath, peeling his palms off the floor, stretching his muscles, arching his back. "You're right," he sighed. "You *are* insane."

He swayed on his feet, savoring each wobble and attempt to balance himself, a dazed smile on his face. "I wonder if she still keeps it in the attic."

"No!" I regained my bearings in the cursed mirror realm and pounded on the closest reflective surface. "Fitz, whatever you're thinking, don't do it. Please. You'll throw this institute into ruin."

He faced the square mirror on the stairwell. "It's already in ruin." And he scurried up to the attic.

I was powerless in the mirror realm, cast in darkness, only seeing light when he passed a reflective surface. One moment I was at the bottom of the stairs, the next I was near Oasis' room, and the next I was in the attic. My muscles tensed beyond my control, and suddenly I was rummaging through the box where she kept Henry and John's belongings. "You don't know what you're doing," I snarled at him through the small hand mirror in the box.

He faced the mirror, clearly expecting to find me there. He flashed me a menacing grin. "I know exactly what I'm doing, *Elliot*."

He pulled out Henry's revolver and checked the chamber. It had only one shot. He smirked into the handheld mirror before closing the box, plunging me into darkness. He knew this wouldn't last for long, and he knew precisely where to go.

Fitz raced to the train station again. The journey was swift. He exited and followed the paths and streets as if he had lived there most of his life, arriving at a charming house in a lovely neighborhood. He peered through its window and saw my horrified reflection. He smiled widely, maliciously. I was helpless.

Fitz knocked. Carew opened.

Shadows enveloped the mirror realm again. I could only hear their voices and the sound of my shallow breath.

"Elliot! Hello. Welcome, come in."

Light entered one corner of the mirror realm. I rushed to it. I saw Fitz through a reflective surface in Anthony's study. He sat in an armchair next to a fancy bookcase, while Fitz occupied the opposite couch. His eyes roamed the room as if following a capricious firefly. They landed on his reflection in Anthony's mirrored bookcase. The smirk he threw me sent a rush of ice clawing down my back.

"So, what's new?" Anthony asked. "How's the study going? The Council is keen for your findings."

"That's exactly why I'm here, Anthony," Fitz replied.

The clock ticked louder than ever. Fitz stood and ambled around the study, examining the area intently, yet naturally. Anthony glanced at the clock—it was 8:13 pm—and grew anxious. He rested his arm on the couch's elegant armrest, his fingers fidgeting. "Can I help you with anything, Elliot?"

Fitz's gaze locked onto Anthony's, who squinted at him. He wandered around the room. "Lovely space," he commented. "Looks expensive." Fitz picked up an umbrella next to the bookcase and patted his palm with it. "How much is it worth? Just this room. I bet you can buy a lot of things with this much money."

Anthony frowned.

"Perhaps you can afford, say..." Fitz squinted one eye, "I don't know, maybe a good number of council members?"

Anthony rose. He began to speak, but Fitz raised a hand and silenced him for the first time in ten years. "No, no, hear me out. I think I'm onto something here. Then *The Conrad* writes this very famous article, one which spreads like wildfire. A fire that perhaps fueled your own purposes and burned Jekyll's. But it fails to mention the bribed council members. Don't you think that's possible?"

"What do you want?" Anthony's eyes flicked to his desk and back to Fitz. "You know what I want." Fitz winked.

"I think it's time for you to leave, Elliot."

"But I just got here," Fitz protested.

"I think you need some rest." Anthony fixed him with a stern gaze. "You're acting strange."

Fitz pursed his lips and raised an eyebrow. Energy bubbled in his chest and pulsed through his arms. I felt it in the mirror realm, ever buzzing and snapping in my peripheries. He smiled at Anthony, then swung his umbrella across his face, knocking him to the ground. In seconds, Fitz was gripping Anthony's neck. My every muscle tensed, and I too lunged and grabbed Anthony's collar as if I were a shadow of Fitz.

"Who are they?" Fitz growled.

"Who are what?" Anthony panted.

"The council members, you bastard. The ones you bribed."

"I bribed?" A snicker escaped him. "I didn't do anything, Elliot. I'm simply trying to do what's best for your precious institute."

"Liar!" Fitz tightened his grip on Anthony's collar with his trembling, yet firm hands, pulling him to his knees. "Last chance, asshole!"

"Or what?" Anthony challenged.

Fitz pulled out the revolver, his murderous eyes speaking for themselves. I struggled in the mirror realm against his will over my body. My arm shook, and I tried to move the revolver away, but my every muscle felt controlled by shadow puppet strings.

Anthony gave a weak cackle. He pulled himself free from Fitz's grip. "You were always fun, Elliot."

Fitz cocked the revolver's hammer.

"So what now, genius?" Anthony put his arms out to the side. "You're going to threaten me. And then what? Wait until the Council finds out about this."

Fitz aimed his revolver at Anthony. He sighed and wiped the blood off his mouth once more before speaking. "Gale Carew. I'm sure your beloved Jekyll told you all about him. Perhaps you even remember."

"How can I forget?" Fitz approached him, the revolver quivering in his grip. "That's the bastard who halted Jekyll's research. The Council was just fine with Jekyll's work. If it wasn't for him, Jekyll would have—"

"That bastard is my father," Anthony interrupted. "But you're right. There was bribery. But I wasn't the one who bribed the Council members, idiot. I barely held a position in the Council."

"Say more."

"Of course, if the bribery was discovered, they would have forced those council members to resign. Not to mention my possible position would be in jeopardy. Great deduction about the article in *The Conrad*, by the way. I thought no one would have guessed." Anthony gave him a silent clap. "Yes. I pulled a few strings to keep my father's actions out of the papers. But guess what? I put you back into the ceremony! So it's all fair and square."

Fitz raised the revolver to Anthony's head. Carew looked down the barrel, visibly sweating, his breath quickening. "We can talk about this, Elliot."

"I'm done talking," Fitz said. "There's more."

Anthony swallowed. Fitz didn't miss the nervous glance Anthony took at his desk. "What's in there? Hmm?" Fitz approached and shook him.

Anthony's mouth quivered, his eyes darting

between Fitz and the desk.

"What's in there, *Carew*?"

"I'm not giving you shit, Elliot," Anthony spat, but Fitz didn't let him finish. He threw Anthony against the wall and forced a fist into his face. I mirrored Fitz's every action, but I would be lying if I said I didn't enjoy Fitz's impulses and mine synchronizing into action.

"Don't call me Elliot." He released his grip on Anthony, who stood on one knee and wiped blood from his nose. He licked a small smudge of blood off his lip before he found himself staring down the revolver again.

"Move," Fitz said. Anthony obeyed. He trudged to his desk.

"Now what?"

"Open it."

Anthony opened the desk.

Fitz aimed his revolver at Anthony and hurried to the desk. Anthony stood his ground, his arms slumped to his sides. Fitz feverishly threw out papers, pens, and trivialities until he found what we both did not expect.

A contract, signed by the insignia of the Council, with three council members' names on it. "Read it." He shoved the contract into Anthony's chest, who drew in a quivering breath and read:

"This contract confirms that Councilmember Anthony G. Carew will oblige to keep the evidence of bribery between his father, Gale Carew, and the three Councilmembers Godfrey Elias, Gemma Rhys, and Curtis Thatcher, under strict confidentiality. The Council allows

Anthony the full clearance to invite The institute of Lysology to the Runeburgh Science and Development Annual Ceremony. In return for Mr. Carew's confidence, the aforementioned Councilmembers will place The institute under Mr. Carew's full supervision; provide 80% of The institute's research grants to Mr. Carew's trusted guidance; sanction royalties from The institute's education and teaching revenue to Mr. Carew; make Mr. Carew the public figure of The institute of Lysology for five years; after which Mr. Carew will be the sole proprietor..."

"...Signed Oct 29-1925, Anthony G. Carew, Councilmember, Godfrey Elias, Gemma Rhys, and Curtis Thatcher," Fitz finished reading, but his eyes still scanned the document. His gaze lifted from the paper to Anthony, who fixed him with a stare. "Those Councilors will be at the Ceremony this year?"

Anthony nodded. "This city's congested with research and development. And there's no hope for your institute to gain the favor of the benefactors it needs. But you found yours." He gestured calmly to himself, as if he wasn't staring down the barrel of a revolver. "I'm bringing Lysology its independence."

"You call this independence?"

"Why, yes. Father was old-fashioned, a true Carew if you ask me. He regarded his enemies as enemies, not as potential allies."

Fitz was at a loss for words, and so was I.

"I mean, if I wasn't able to use my father's mistake to my advantage and blackmail those council members into placing Lysology under my sole supervision and control, how else would Lysology see the light of day? I'm doing you a favor, trust me." He had the nerve to wink at Fitz. "So you found the evidence. Now what?"

"Does the Council know?"

"Of course they do! I'm the one who convinced the Head Councilor to reinstate the good Council members and invite your institute." Anthony shrugged.

"Not the reinstatement, you bastard. The contract!" Fitz raised his revolver in Anthony's face.

Anthony raised an eyebrow and swallowed. "No. Head Councilor Alexi Clarckson is a busy man. He need not know of those details."

Fitz secured the contract in his pockets before Anthony could grasp it. He aimed his revolver at Anthony's head and walked closer. Anthony raised his hands. I sensed his fear. I could almost smell it. Taste it in this realm. It was quite appetizing.

"I could kill you," Fitz said. "Right now. But that won't do me, Oasis, or the institute any good, now will it?" He put the barrel to Anthony's temple. Anthony shook his head, his eyes almost closed. "Listen, Councilmember. If you even think of spreading news or in any way jeopardizing the institute and my work, I can easily request the Council for an investigation into your father's bribery and your own blackmail." He shook the contract vehemently in front of Anthony's quivering face. Anthony swallowed down his words. "And they won't have a hard time finding the evidence. I'm sure Elliot will be more than willing to cooperate. For once."

He was right. "That's what now, *genius*," Fitz said and made for the door.

The streets of Runeburgh blurred around him. When he reached our institute, I regained control. I staggered past the gates, through the garden, and into the building, rushing to my bedroom and closing the door. With both hands on the door, I hung my head and breath fell heavy from my chest. And he was back in the mirror again.

Egoveritas was strong, incredibly strong. It threw me and Fitz into the mirror with the same violence as it tore us out of it. Neither of us had experienced anything like this with Nafs. I removed my waistcoat and tossed it into the bathroom. Lightning flashed outside my window, followed by a distant rumble of thunder. The rain fell in small flecks on my window, then poured after another flash of lightning and a crash of thunder.

I showered, and the mirror fogged up. I wiped it and looked at my reflection. It was still me. I left the bathroom and closed the door behind me. The rain poured down, drumming against my window.

I turned the long, broken mirror upright. "You ruined us." I turned the mirror to face me, and I stared at my shattered reflection. "You are a psychopath. You are a maniac!" I paced my room, my fists clenched and cold. I glanced at the ring box and opened it. The jewel taunted me. I became aware of insight, so sharp and bright, that I had to look away from the mirror. I wanted to speak to it, to speak to Fitz. But I couldn't face my reflection. I scrambled for the cloth and covered the mirror.

"I wouldn't have known about this contract if you hadn't—" I rubbed my face and sat at the edge of my bed, exhaustion suddenly settling on my shoulders. I addressed the silenced

mirror again. "I'm so stupid. I could have led our institute into the hands of a damned Carew. I'm such a coward."

I held the box and the contract in my lap and lay down in bed, sleepless. Thoughts, routes, and plans murmured in my head.

My experience with Egoveritas sparked an idea. If Egoveritas is strong enough to pull him out of the mirror with such acuity, it should be strong enough to confine him to the mirror as well. I had enough time to experiment before the Ceremony, and enough time to figure out what to do with this damned contract.

I closed my eyes.

He saw every fleeting thought in my mind, heard every word I said. I could see him standing in the void of the mirror realm, bathed in fear and anguish. And when I was sure of that, I finally fell asleep.

Atonement

I have been living on little sleep, whatever salty snacks I could scavenge, and a steady supply of sour drinks, such as wine and gin, and lots of Egoveritas.

I was unaware of hunger or fatigue, and I devoted my time to the lab, having lost track of time since the incident with Anthony.

All I knew was the number of weeks remaining until the Ceremony.

And I had seven weeks left.

My hands moved with expert precision, my mind adept at determining the reagents. This formula would make a shell out of him. I poured the 60 centiliters into a vial, the final purple crystals of Egoveritas winking out into the purple liquid as the solution settled.

I consumed the first third of the potion, and I felt my veins ignite. My knuckles turned white as I clutched the flask, hunching over to cradle my contorting abdomen. I held on tight, tighter, until the pain became tolerable. Trembling, I stood upright and took another gulp.

I placed the flask on the bench before my grip failed and faced the reflective cabinet glass. "Come on," I urged my reflection, my green eyes staring back. "Come on!" I downed the remaining potion, bile rising in my throat.

My reflection remained unchanged. Despite my desperate attempts to will him through, I was the only one in the mirror. I screamed and hurled the empty vial across the lab. Oasis' voice from one of my many nightmares echoed in my head. *You're sick, Elliot.* "You're right." I removed my glasses and tossed them onto the bench. "I am sick." I slumped onto the bench seat, suddenly feeling the crushing weight of loss. The weight enveloped my chest, back, and shoulders like a damp blanket.

You're sick, Elliot.

You're a coward.

I hurried to prepare another dose, thoughts and memories swirling as a backdrop to my mechanical actions. I knocked back another 60 centiliters, a searing pain piercing my chest and radiating through my limbs. For a moment, I was aware of nothing but the reflective surfaces in the room and the winding, twisting agony.

Shakily, I faced my reflection, compelled by an unseen force.

Red irises stared back at me. All it took was 60 centiliters.

I approached the cabinet and placed my hands on the surface, cracks and fissures etched into my parched knuckles. The reflection mirrored mine, save for the irises. In a fleeting moment, I saw his eyes brimming with tears. I blinked, and the eyes gazing back at me were dry again. I blinked once more, and I could have sworn my younger self was smiling back at me. Another blink, and I faced those chilling red eyes.

The reflection grinned, something deranged, yet endearing. "You've made me do something I've *long* held in my heart." I pulled away from the reflection, a crazed smile crossing my face. "If only I could just—" I wrung my hands together, envisioning Anthony's neck within my grasp, "do it again. But I can't." I gestured toward the cabinet window. "I was out of control. I *hate* being out of control." I sauntered over to the flask and inhaled its aroma. I could still smell the saltiness, feel the sting tantalizing my every nerve. I relished it.

A muffled howl resonated in my ears, making me flinch.

He was screaming inside my head.

I hastened to concoct another 60 centiliters to silence him, ignoring the reflection as he pounded on the window while I worked. My trembling hands poured the salts, disregarding measurements. His voice became a siren in my mind. The solution bubbled.

He screamed again, this time his voice clearer. He hammered on the glass. I didn't wait for the solution to cool before forcing it down my throat, swallowing back the churning sensation in my stomach.

Suddenly, all was quiet. Breathing heavily, I stared at the red irises of my reflection. The eyes were his, but the control was mine. A grin split across my face, quietude in my mind. I had discovered the threshold of control.

Punishment

I perceived time only through the seconds I counted in my mind, the thumps I heard in my ears, and the sporadic bursts of pain that stabbed at me.

The pain arrived in intervals, Elliot's intervals. Morning, evening, and night, I assumed. With each drink, my peripheral vision darkened, my head spun, and his control tightened. Breathing became a struggle. Each breath grew heavier, each exhale forced, each aimless, hollow step burdened. The institute in the mirror realm appeared desolate, dark, and silent, enveloped by an oppressive air that constricted my lungs and smothered my consciousness. I came to a halt in my room. I sat down on the bed, feeling the pillows, but it was so dark. I could barely discern the outlines of my hands, my bed, or the door.

It was so empty and unbearably cold...

I felt foreign, unwelcome, as if my bed was retching my body away. Suddenly, my senses were overwhelmed.

He took another one again...

The lights snapped on, searing my eyes. I shielded my face from the harsh light. When my eyes adjusted to the light, I found myself in the lab, facing the cabinets. Elliot stood on the other side of the glass, grinning manically.

I lunged at him, but collided with something.

Glass.

I pounded on it.

Chunks of reality and unreality blended into a living nightmare.

Pain and light flashed within and around me. My breath caught in my throat, and the pain and light vanished as quickly as they had appeared. He materialized in the mirror again, a ring of red and black encircling his eyes, stubble sprouting on his face. Light flashed once more.

Elliot stood closer to the mirror, brandishing a vial. He smiled. He wanted me to see this. He flicked the vial and drank up, plunging me back into the void.

Time passed.

Seconds. Minutes. Hours. Days.

Intervals of piercing pain and desperate gasps for air.

"Elliot, let me out!" Suddenly, I was pounding on the shadowy glass of a mirror, unable to see even my own reflection.

There was nothing. It was so cold, so quiet. Please, someone.

My head is killing me, my knees ached, and I collapsed onto the dark, carpeted floor shrouded in shadows. I curled up like a child. A bitter sob tore through my throat. I wept and wept, taking a breath only to release it in another sob. I could taste it in my mouth.

Egoveritas. So bitter so acrid. I retched and coughed. The substance felt thick, enveloping my limbs like mud. I remained curled on the floor, one hand holding my hair, the other lying palm down on the void of the ground.

Here, in the dying echo of the mirror realm, memories and thoughts descended on me like dust motes. My hand lifted weakly. Under a spotlight, dust continued to fall like thick snow. Loneliness burdened me, guilt gnawing at every corner of my chest.

But if only Elliot had given Nafs a chance. If only he had been more patient. If only Oasis hadn't hidden the letter.

If only I hadn't jeopardized the institute with my outburst.

Then perhaps I wouldn't be buried in dust and isolation.

"Maybe I deserve it." A whisper slipped out, quiet and pitiful. I was being punished. My father punished me. My mother punished me. Oasis punished me.

It made sense that Elliot would punish me, too.

"It's so easy. I could give up right now. I could sleep. Is that what you want?" I turned my tearful, blurry gaze towards where I thought the mirror was. I was certain he could hear me. "I could sleep for the last time." I closed my eyes, ready for eternal slumber to release me.

Surrendering my will would be the ultimate punishment. That thought consumed me, filled my fading existence.

My eyes flew open when another wave of pain

seized me, droplets of salty tears splashing onto my thumb, and something dragged me into a seat, facing a covered mirror.

Repentance

I uncovered the mirror in my room. I hadn't been up here in days, sleeping on the benches or in the guest room after long, timeless hours in the lab, perfecting the formula. Dust had gathered on every surface. I ran my finger over the nightstand, lifting a trail of dust until I reached the handle. I opened it, pulled out a vial, and found Anthony's contract.

"So." I uncovered the mirror and sat facing it, the contract in my lap, the vial of sixty four centiliters of Egoveritas between my fingers. I gazed at my reflection: green irises, a stubble that had grown into a beard, and a mop of hair that sorely needed combing. "Let's try this again." I drank thirty-two centiliters of it, hissing as it burned down my throat and made my stomach churn.

He hissed as well, buzzing in the periphery of my ears that turned into the squeal of steam, and funneled into a scream. The voice refocused into the mirror. The irises turned red, and my reflection's features shifted from cold indifference to hot panic.

"The amount you're consuming—" his voice came from the mirror, tuning in and out like a radio.

"*It's absurd.*"

"I thought you liked Egoveritas."

"*Not in these quantities. It's choking me.*"

"Good." I gazed back at that set of eyes. I saw innocence. I saw heartbreak and heartache. I saw Fitz. "You're going to Shift in the Ceremony."

"*Like hell I will—*"

I brought the vial to my lips as a threat. He recoiled in terror. The formula had a tight grip on him. "You're going to Shift in the Ceremony on my terms. I will you in, and I will you out. I will clear my name and regain the institute's reputation. I need to fix this mess you made."

"*What about your mess?*" He leaned toward me. "*Who's going to clean that up?*"

I glanced at the vial in my hands and swallowed. I tried to deny it, forcing a coolness into my voice. "What mess?" He didn't question me. He knew I was lying to myself. To both of us.

"*The mess between you and me. The one you made the moment you left London for Runeburgh. You forgot all about me.*"

"What is there to remember?"

He lunged in his seat, a tremor in his voice. "*Fitz Garrison.*" He gestured to himself, a weak, agitated laughter breaking his words. "*Elliot left him to die in London. And never thought to pay him a visit.*" His words silenced mine. I tried to speak, but tears crumbled my voice. All I could manage to do was nod. He continued. "*I just wanted to set things right between the both of us. There was so much, too much, you left behind in London. And I tried to make you remember it. But you silenced me with this.*" He shot a pained look at the vial in my hands.

I nodded again, tears falling from my eyes. My voice emerged frail and heavy. "You're right. I thought I could bury everything that happened to you in London before I became Elliot in Runeburgh. I wanted to start anew. And I succeeded for years. I hid you from everyone, including Oasis, for so long. Until I tasted this cursed formula."

"*Then release me.*"

"We're not what's important now!" I shouted. "All I care about is the institute and Oasis." Twisting the vial in my hand, I released a trembling breath. "I'll worry about you and me after the Ceremony. You could have cost us the institute."

He sank into his seat, a sudden burden weighing down his features. "*When I saw Anthony controlling the institute, controlling you and Oasis like that... I don't know what got into me.*" What little vitality he had left diminished in his reflection, and he appeared like a marionette abandoned in a chair, left to gather dust. "*I deserve this. I'm sorry,*" he said.

"You fucked up." I sat back in my seat, exhaustion settling in. He seemed to acknowledge his responsibility, and I became cognizant of mine. "We all did. I did. Oasis did." I found it in my heart to pity him. To pity us. "When Oasis hid my mother's passing from me, I had to make sure I silenced you more. I'm sorry."

Silence fell between us, interrupted only by the wind outside, the ticking clock, and the creaking of my window.

"*What are you planning to do with this?*" he nodded to the paper in my lap, his movements slow, his face sullen, his voice coarse.

I looked at the contract Fitz recklessly stole from Anthony with a hungry vengeance I ached to satisfy. "I don't know. He's a Carew. He could throw the institute into ruin if he wants." I cupped my face, my elbows resting on my knees. "I *have* to succeed in the Ceremony. I'm terrified, Fitz. I'm terrified."

"*I am too.*"

His words rested heavily in my heart. Silence overcame my room. I heard him shift in his seat through the mirror.

"*But it is strange that he hasn't sent the authorities to the institute by now, after my little rampage,*" he said.

I sat back in my seat, frowning. Fitz was right. It's been weeks. Anthony hasn't said a word. I lifted the contract. He's afraid they will find his dirty secret.

"*Take it with you,*" Fitz said. I faced the mirror and locked eyes with him. "*Might come in handy in the presentation. There's no reason you can't play dirty, too.*"

For once, I kept my eyes on the mirror, holding my gaze on him. I folded the contract and tucked it into my pocket. Sleep danced in my eyes. I stood and opened the vial. The second half would cast him into darkness, and the solution would cut its way through my veins, kneading my heart. I could not face him while I drank the rest. I reached to cover the mirror.

"One more thing."

I stopped.

"What are you going to do with the ring?"

"I'm taking that with me as well."

"You better shape up before then." His voice was barely audible. I nodded and covered the mirror, hesitance finding its way into my hands for once.

I opened the drawer and set the ring box between the stashes of smuggled Egoveritas. I drank the second half of the formula in slow sips, allowing Fitz the mercy to dissipate back into the mirror at his own pace. It was painful still, but not as brutal. I curled up in my bed and surrendered to sleep.

Mending

The formula was complete, just as I needed it. The transformation was difficult, and the anguish was far from being remedied, but I would worry about that after the Ceremony. I considered my relationship with Fitz mended. But I had one more important relationship to heal. So important, in fact, that I cleaned myself up, shaved, and dressed well. I looked in the mirror. My face looked somber. I was a shell dressed in a well-tailored suit, carrying a bouquet and a ring box.

The train stopped, and I left the station, walking down the charming, beautiful street that I still remembered fondly. I saw the house in the distance. A smile revealed my nostalgia. I used to live here with Uncle John, Henry, and Oasis, sharing laughs, tears, breakfasts, and gifts— compasses, scarves, and magnets. I clutched the bouquet of poppies, lilies, and roses in my hand as if holding onto a lifeline. I knocked on the door.

Silence.

Then the door opened. She appeared. I released a trembling breath. "Oasis."

"Elliot," she said, her voice gentle and cautious.

"I, uh—" I fumbled, "how are you?"

"I'm all right. You?"

"Good."

"It's cold outside. Come in." She walked inside, and I followed. Every step I took resonated within me, stirring memories I had longed to recall. We sat in the living room where I first met Oasis, sipping Uncle John's warm soup, my frame shivering by the fireplace after three long days of cold and hunger. I could feel our past selves, our past souls, still lingering, attached to the couches, chairs, and the mantle clock.

I extended the bouquet to her. "This is for you."

She held it gingerly and took a sniff. She smiled, but her smile faded as quickly as it had formed, as though she couldn't allow herself a moment of joy.

The mantle clock ticked and clicked, and I struggled to find the right words. Finally, I spoke. "Our institute can present at the Ceremony. We have another chance. I–I fixed the formula. I just want to make things right for us."

She looked at me over the bouquet. "How?"

"I had the best teacher," I said. "You." A long silence stretched between us before I leaned in and held her face in my hands. "Oasis, please. Come back. I—I can't attend the Ceremony without you. I can't—I can't be in the institute without you. It feels barren and quiet and—"

She set the bouquet aside and pressed her lips into mine, silencing me. We hungered for each other, our kiss searching and finding something only to lose it and find it again. We parted, and she rested her forehead against mine, our noses almost touching. "I'm so sorry for treating you like a fragile thing, Elliot. Please forgive me."

"I am sorry. I never meant to say what I did. I was—"

"Forgive me," she repeated.

"Come back to me."

She embraced me. "I will." She let out a soft giggle. "I will."

I allowed myself to sink into her embrace, and a sense of peace that I hadn't experienced in the past few months washed over me. I closed my eyes and savored it for once.

The Ceremony

The fateful night arrived. The Ceremony was to take place at Glass Plaza. A beam of light entered the void in one corner. Fitz crawled towards it. I unveiled my tall mirror and examined myself. My face revealed the ordeal he and I had endured, but I concealed it beneath my formal attire and clean-shaven countenance. He watched me adjust my tie in the mirror. I don't like ties. I prefer bowties. We both did. I don't know why I didn't wear one.

Fitz was unaware of my actions behind the concealed mirrors. Yet he experienced every grueling moment. The fervor and violence with which I had consumed Egoveritas leading up to the Ceremony strained the mirror realm, leaving Fitz a mere shadow of himself. Any slight pressure could shatter the realm and Fitz along with it. I drew in a shaky breath before covering the mirror again. Behind the veil, he heard me pop a vial and drink.

With Anthony's contract, the ring box, and two vials in my pocket, I descended the stairs. My heart leaped at the sight of Oasis. She awaited me at the entrance, donning a stunning suit, a flower nestled in her hair's ringlets. "Ready?"

"Of course," I replied as I joined her.

"Where's your bowtie?" She playfully touched my jaw before poking at my tie. "I don't know," I admitted.

"You'll have to show me how you look in a bowtie after the Ceremony, then." I smiled, clutching the ring box in my pocket. "I'll indeed have to show you. I owe you." We exited the institute and linked arms. Taking the train, we arrived at the reception

within an hour. I could hear the chatter of the crowd, sense the lights shine, the wine sting, the air tense with anticipation for *The institute of Lysology's* revival. All the sensation was just beyond Fitz's reach.

Anthony, clad in his costly jacket and holding a glass of champagne, was unmistakable among the crowd. He conversed smoothly with his colleagues. Smiling, he approached us. "Congratulations." He handed me a glass of champagne and sipped from his own. "You made it."

I held the glass and took a sip.

"Come on, Elliot," he said, draping his arm over my shoulders. "Look at all these people. And look at the council members over there." He gestured towards them with his glass. "They're all waiting, *rooting* for you." He leaned close to my ear and whispered, his voice venomous, "Release that contract, and I will make sure your little institute never sees the light of day again." He pulled away and flashed me a smile. "Give us a good show."

I shuffled myself from his arm and took another

sip. A deep rage stirred within Fitz, and I could feel it. The heat was suffocating. It solidified into something tangible and heavy, pushing against the glass barrier that Egoveritas had put between us.

Ladies and gentlemen, may I present to you Elliot Warlow and Oasis Utterson's Lysology.

I cleared my throat. "We're up."

Oasis and I ascended the stairs to the stage, the audience below looked like ants gathered around crumbs. From my vantage point, I saw Anthony join the Council members, his champagne half-empty, his smile poisonous.

"Thank you all for coming," Oasis began. "We acknowledge the hesitance that all of Runeburgh holds toward Lysology. That's why we wanted to express our gratitude for your open-mindedness."

It was my turn. I attempted to steady my gaze, my eyes shifting between the massive crowd and the Council. "We wish to express our gratitude to the esteemed Councilmember Anthony Carew for his—" I swallowed hard, struggling to continue my speech, "his invaluable assistance and support. Our journey here was fraught with challenges, and without the consideration of Runeburgh's Science and Development Council, we would not have made it."

Oasis spoke next. "The focus of our study was to explore Shifting. Through Shifting, we aim to gain a better understanding of one of the most complex phenomena in our world." Two mirrors flanked me, angled in such a way that the crowd could see. I carefully took out the first vial. Silence fell over the

Glass Plaza like honey.

"This is the modified formula that my father, Dr. Jekyll, created to access his soul. His pioneering research was in its infancy, and Elliot and I have refined the formula in a way that bridges the connection between our realm..." She gestured toward one of the mirrors, "and our souls."

The silence ballooned, leaving me to listen to the murmurs and rumblings in my head, my bones grinding with the sound of glass cracking. The first dose of the formula would release him. I braced myself, uncorked the vial, and drank.

I was accustomed to the formula's salty bitterness, and I managed to swallow it without a grimace. I recorked the vial and showed the empty container to the audience. As the formula coursed through my system, the heat dissipated, the pressure eased, and his whispers vanished. I turned to the mirror. My reflection blinked once, then twice. The irises transformed to a vibrant red. I clasped my hands behind my back.

Fitz, now visible in the mirror, turned to the audience and bowed. The crowd erupted in applause, amused chatter rippling through the assembly below the stage. I locked eyes with Fitz, crumpling Anthony's contract in my pocket. I returned Anthony's suave smile. Some Councilmembers scribbled notes, while others whispered amongst themselves.

"Fascinating," Councilmember Gemma Rhys said, not lifting her eyes from her papers. She turned to her colleagues. "Any comments?"

Curtis Thatcher spoke up. "What direction does the institute of Lysology plan to take with this formula next?"

"We plan to refine it further," Oasis answered. "We will need to conduct multiple trials of the same experiment. We hope the Council will authorize research that allows Shifting to become a trusted method for studying the soul."

"What salts are in use?" Godfrey inquired.

"Nafs," Oasis quickly replied. "We hope our institute can advance research with newer, more efficient salts. However, our findings indicate the salts aren't the key to the success of this endeavor."

"Then what is?" Godfrey Elias muttered.

"The individual's willingness to participate," Fitz answered. The crowd murmured among themselves, while the Councilmembers exchanged whispers.

My ear fizzled with Fitz's voice.

The contract. Show them.

A cough crept into my chest, and I held the second vial tightly in my pocket. I heard pounding in my head, something muffled behind glass. The sound of glass cracking filled my ears. I couldn't ignore it, and part of me didn't want to. **Crick**

I hid a wince.

"A very promising demonstration," Godfrey said. "This could indeed steer Runeburgh's scientific advancements in new directions."

Crack

Anthony spoke next. "I am very eager for us to

collaborate, Mr. Warlow, Ms. Utterson." He flashed me a glance. I turned to Fitz, who offered another bow, drawing further amusement from the crowd.

My vision blurred, and a hissing sound filled my ears. A sudden heat fumed in my head. The roaring of a fire and the shriek of steam filled my mind. I keeled over, a searing pain gripping my heart. I grunted, clutching my chest. Soft whispers fluttered across the crowd. "Elliot?" Oasis touched my shoulder.

Then I heard him inside my head, screaming, roaring, pounding against the glass barrier that separated my mind from my body. Pressure built inside my head. My skin felt as if it were being stretched like the surface of a mirror, bent into shapes it was not made for. I fumbled for another vial to douse him in another dose and plunge him to silence.

But I couldn't.

CRACK

The contract.

I spilled the contents of the second vial, leaving my will exposed to Fitz's whims. And the glass barrier between us shattered. My mind spiraled and fell, and Fitz, my soul, and my body's strength plummeted with it. Fitz was tearing through me, invading my will. I reeled against the railings, a scream building in my chest.

"Elliot?" Oasis' trembling voice came from behind me. All I could hear was the whistling steam, the roaring fire, the grinding of glass against soul against mind against body against glass. My heart pounded in my ears. A scream escaped me. The crowd gasped and murmured in response.

Oasis dropped to my side. "What's happening?" She cupped my cheeks in her hands, but I was too busy gasping for air to answer. The two mirrors shattered, splintering Fitz's image. A wave of disbelief swept over the audience. Another scream escaped me as Fitz ripped through. I closed my green eyes, and when they opened, his red irises met Oasis' gaze.

He knew time was running out. He sprang to his feet and lunged at Anthony, pinning him against the railing. The crowd beneath gasped in unison at the sight. The onslaught of sensations overwhelmed his consciousness. The lights blinded his eyes, the sweet scent of delectable food and wine tantalized his nostrils. Fitz grinned. There was absolution in chaos.

"Ladies and gentlemen," he shouted. I listened. "There's no need for alarm. This is all part of the act." He pressed Anthony against the railing. "Mr. Carew, before we finalize our agreements, would you mind telling Mr. Clarkson about the blackmail?"

A buzz arose among the audience.

"Blackmail?" Clarkson peered at us over his spectacles.

Anthony glared into Fitz's murderous eyes. "Elliot, what are you doing?"

"Don't call me Elliot!" Fitz roared. He paused, as though deciding how to deliver the final blow. He released Anthony and turned to Clarkson, placing the contract on the table in one swift motion.

Clarkson frowned, his bushy eyebrows furrowing over incredulous eyes as he scanned the document.

He turned to the Councilmembers on his right. "This is highly concerning, Mr. Carew," he rasped.

Oasis rushed to Fitz's side. She recognized those red irises. "What is this?"

"I'll explain soon," he stammered, leaning on Oasis' arm for support.

"Mr. Clarkson, sir," Anthony moved away from the railing. "You can't believe this man's allegations. He's—" He glared in Fitz's direction, "he's clearly delusional. It must be the experiments. I will see to it that this doesn't happen again. Under my supervision, I will ensure that—"

"The evidence suggests otherwise," Clarkson interjected.

"Mr. Clarkson—"

"Sit, Mr. Carew." His voice echoed across the Glass Plaza's open hall, silencing the whispers among the crowd. He turned to the three Councilmembers in question. Some averted their gaze, while others shot Anthony a fiery glance. "We will attend to this matter after the Ceremony."

Anthony sat down.

The ground vanished beneath my feet in the realm, and I fell, plummeting back into my body. Our soul disintegrated, our minds crumbled, and our body weakened. Fitz clawed at his chest. Oasis clutched his hand and led us down the stairs. He glanced behind her, searching for any sign of Anthony's presence. "While you were away, I took control of Elliot's body—"

"What?" Her voice was a heated whisper, guiding us away from the presentations. We arrived in the lobby, security already gathering at the heart of the Plaza, our presence lost among the crowd and chaos.

"I threatened Anthony. Hear me out." He gripped her elbows, his knees shaking, his will fading. "Anthony's father bribed those very councilmembers. You remember him? Gale?" She nodded, and Fitz took another glance behind her before continuing. "His bribery led to the banning of Uncle Jekyll's research. I found this contract in Anthony's quarters—" When her eyes widened in shock, he cupped her cheek. "I fucked up, I know. But Anthony was blackmailing those councilmembers to gain control of our institute." He fumbled with his words, his voice frail with a tremor. "Elliot couldn't stand having our institute under a Carew's control. I couldn't stand having a Carew controlling my life again, and I—"

"When did this happen?"

"While you were away. I'm—I'm sorry. Elliot was drinking Egoveritas, and—"

"Egoveritas? How much?" Oasis rushed through her words. Anthony was treading in our direction. Oasis shook me. "Fitz! How much?"

"Sixty-four. I don't know, maybe three, four times a day—" Agony surged through him. He grunted and dropped to one knee.

"Sixty!" Her voice was breathless. "That's too much. This is…" She struggled to catch her breath. "This is bad. We have to get you back home." She held his hand and prepared to rush us out of the Plaza. "We have to contact Dr. Amy. She'll—"

Anthony intercepted us and separated Oasis and

me. He grabbed Fitz's shoulder and lifted him to his feet. "I will end your institute. You insignificant ant."

Oasis landed a solid fist on Anthony's face. "Fuck off."

Elliot, Fitz, or whoever it was now, staggered alongside Oasis. She frantically bolted through the doors and lead us to the train station.

Sleep

In an instant, she wrapped my arm around her shoulder. The next moment, I found myself on a train, and soon after, I was dragging my feet towards our institute.

My legs couldn't carry me any further. "Oasis, wait. Stop—" I swayed on my knees. "I can't breathe." I fell at the entrance, Oasis cradling me gently.

A sob stole her breath away. "Oh God, I've killed you."

"Oasis—"

She brushed a lock of hair from my eye. "I shouldn't have left you alone."

"Oasis—"

"You'll be okay. I promise—"

"Oasis!" I cried, the effort to speak draining me. I continued in a near whisper. "Listen." I brought a trembling hand to her face and stroked her cheek. "Help me up."

"Where?"

"Up the stairs. I don't want to propose in a tie."

"What?"

I was already wobbling on my knees, pain

blossoming through my joints.

She supported me. "Elliot, what are you doing?"

I took the first step, sweat beading on my neck from the exertion. "Just—trust me." I continued climbing the stairs. Each step was a mountain, each breath a dagger. My legs moved, my back arching with tension and agony. Pain demanded my attention. I felt Fitz and I both inside and outside the realm at once. My vision dimmed, but I kept my eyes open enough to see the next step.

"I don't know what's going to happen to the institute. I'm—I'm sorry," I uttered between grunts.

"That's not what's important right now," she replied. I nearly missed a step, and she gripped my elbow, steadying my feet. "We need to get you out of Runeburgh. Dr. Amy will know what to do."

"No time…" My words came out as a weak trill as we finally reached my bedroom. Clinging to Oasis' arm, I shakily moved to my closet and fumbled for a bowtie. I kept tens of them. I didn't know which one I grabbed. I staggered to the long mirror, Oasis supporting my unsteady steps. Pain surged in my stomach and spread to my chest. I clenched the cloth covering the mirror, but my legs gave out. I fell, the cloth falling with me, revealing the mirror that framed us. I glanced at my reflection. Fitz and I were dying.

"Can you—help me put this on?" I presented her with the bowtie.

Oasis held it as if it were a precious jewel. She cradled me again and pulled me close. The sudden movement sent a wild pang through my abdomen that ended in a scream. "I'm sorry! I'm sorry…" she softened her grip on me.

I moved my neck for Oasis, a hiss escaping my throat. I nestled back down, pressure building in my temples and shoulders, seeping into my chest. Her hands trembled as she worked with the cloth. I exhaled in relief as she secured the bowtie in place.

"There," Oasis sniffed and patted the bowtie. Her mouth quivered, her eyes filled with tears. They fell on my cheeks, and she wiped them away. I smiled and closed my eyes. Something soothed my shrinking consciousness, lulling me closer to sleep. "You look dashing," she said.

I mustered a smile.

"What's going to happen?" she whispered, her voice choked with emotion. "I don't know…"

"I'll fix this." She shifted her legs, preparing to lift me up. "Lie down in bed. Hang on. I'll get you to Dr. Amy. Maybe—maybe we can do something with my father's brew." She tried to pull away, but I clung to her and shook my head.

"I think I'm dying…"

She shook her head, her voice breaking with a shaky breath. "No. No, you're not. You're not dying, Elliot."

"It really feels like it, though."

Fitz's voice echoed in the mirror. With a small gasp, Oasis turned to it. I strained my neck towards the mirror, a cough seizing me.

"Show her the ring," he wheezed. In the mirror, Fitz patted his breast pocket. I reached for her hand and

tenderly kissed it before guiding it to my chest. She found her way into the pocket and pulled out the box, opening it.

"The jeweler said Uncle Utterson bought his wedding ring there." I tried to smile, but managed only a wince. Tears welled up in her eyes and nose. She sniffed and wiped them away. "Oasis Utterson. What a beautiful name," I said. "Will you marry me?"

She sniffed, her thumb gently rubbing the side of my eye. "Yes."

"All of me. Fitz and Elliot alike."

"Yes," she chuckled, tears breaking through her laughter. "Yes."

I smiled weakly. "Great."

"Great," she echoed.

She drew close to me, and we kissed. There was innocence lost and innocence reborn. I felt as though I had finally released him, my soul—something science could not explain. I had no desire to explain it.

I fell asleep. The last thing I remember was the sensation of her lips on mine.

Epilogue

I did not know how long I held him and rocked, quietly weeping into his limp neck. "I'm so sorry," I murmured. My lips quivered as I pulled away, brushing a strand of red hair off his sweaty forehead. My hand found his bowtie and I rubbed the fabric. "The color matches your eyes, Elliot." My voice was faint when I addressed him. "It's quite charming. You're— you're charming." I sniffed and took a long look at him, committing his every feature to my memory: his pale freckles that dotted his high cheekbones and subtle nose, his closed eyelids that hooded his eyes, his slim lips ever so slightly parted. But his image blurred in my vision when my eyes filled up with relentless tears. I pulled him back to me, nuzzling his head in my shoulder.

The engagement ring on my finger jabbed my arm when I pressed us close. It daunted me, scolding me for what I have done, what I should have and could have done. Images of my father's passing rushed through my memories, unearthing sorrow, and anguish from the depths of my mind like buried roots. The last year of his life was fraught with delirium and fever, cravings and nightmares, and the pains of shifting between the mirror. Elliot and Fitz have experienced in weeks what my father had experienced in a whole year.

Except father had the support of his family, of us. Elliot had no one. I left him. "Forgive me," I sighed, a tear slipping from my closed eyes. I wished for Elliot to stir in my arms, to press a hand to my cheek, to tell me he forgives me. I wished for Fitz to say something witty from the other side of the mirror. "You're right. I am sick. I'm sorry I hid the letter from you. I'm sorry I left you. I love you." I glanced at the mirror, a sense of displacement sweeping over me. "All of you. Fitz and Elliot alike. Say *great*, please," I whispered. But I was surrounded by silence.

I remembered the paper Fitz placed on Clarckson's desk and Anthony's threat, but my heart was too full of grief to think of what that was all about. A sudden crushing heaviness weighed me down. I closed my eyes and pressed his forehead against mine, his skin still feverish, wishing we could speak and relieve each other of our troubles. "I can't run this institute alone." I pressed his forehead to mine, and fresh tears spilled over my face. I gasped when I heard something. I put my ear close to his nose.

Breath! I heard breath! Shallow and precious, delicate against my skin. I drew his arm around my shoulder, puffing as I stood and dragged him up with me. I set him down on the bed and pulled his legs over the covers. Brushing my hair away from my ears, I listened close again. His breath was thin and infrequent.

Frenzy captured me, and I rushed to my room,

grabbing a bag and tossing a garment into it. I dug through my desk and crowded important documents I thought I needed to get us out of Runeburgh. I bolted back to his wardrobe and packed three bowties into it.

"I'm going to get us out of here before Anthony does anything rash," I said to the mirror, hoping Fitz and Elliot could hear me. "You'll have to forgive me. I'm leaving the institute behind."

I threw a few of his garments into the bag, the contents in utter chaos before I was back at his side on the bed. I cupped his clammy cheeks and pressed his nose to mine. I took my time, as though everything in the world was as it should be. "We will build something new together, all right?" I said quietly, as though not to disturb his sleep, and brushed the side of his eye, my thumb coming away damp with his feverish skin. "We will rebuild this institute. Somewhere far away from here. Away from this insane city. Where we can flourish together. All right?"

The doorbell to the institute rang and I pulled away, breathless, tears drying on my face. "Oh no." My heart raced and pounded in my ears. Thoughts swarmed my mind like flies. *It could be the Council authorities. The police. Anthony could be out there.* The doorbell rang again.

They're going to take him from me.

But he's still breathing.

He's dying.

They're going to take him—

I shook my head, wiped the tears off my face, and took a shivering breath as I faltered to the entrance.

I faced the door, my shoulders tense as ice. My hand quivered over the doorknob. I closed my eyes, braced myself, and opened.

"Hello, Oasis."

Tension fell from my shoulders like an avalanche.

"Dr. Amy! Thank God it's you!" Ease found its way into my panicked voice as I clasped her arms. Her aged features could not hide the concerned gaze I was so used to in my youth.

"I came to Runeburgh as soon as I found out you were presenting. I saw what happened in the Ceremony. Where's Elliot?" Dr. Amy balanced me as she entered the institute. She was the only thing keeping me from collapsing under my feet.

"Upstairs." I closed the door hastily behind her, grateful that it was her and no one else. "I've perfected the remedy we gave Henry, Egomora—you remember it. It should be able to stabilize Elliot for now."

"We need to get him out of Runeburgh."

Dr. Amy stopped and turned to me. "But Oasis, dear," she looked around her, "what of the institute?"

"I'll worry about that later," I confessed.

"What about Anthony? Elliot revealed something Anthony clearly did not want to be revealed. I doubt he has good intentions for—"

"That's not what's important right now!" I nearly shouted. I caught my breath, speaking quietly next. "I'm sorry. Please. He's—he's all I have." I gazed at her with pleading eyes. She held my shaking hands, stilling them for a moment. I released a breath and sniffed when she tucked my hair behind my ear.

"I have one vial handy; we need to get this to him fast. But that won't be the end of it. We need to get you both out of Runeburgh."

"Where? We can't go to London. It's not safe for him there."

"Not London. Porto Dell' Armonia."

Acknowledgments

Rima, my sister, my biggest number one fan. My first reader, and the first person to whom I dedicate this story. This story and every story I write and share is dedicated to you. Every one of my stories hereafter will acknowledge you, your unconditional love and care, and your innocent passion and devotion. I love you.

To my mother, who sacrificed so much and dared to dream and do. Without you, I would not have the time and space needed to write, grow and share this story.

To the person who knows me by the nickname ShamShooMee. I'd be deep in the trenches without you. Thank you.

To my workshop buddies! Thank you for helping me workshop and revise Doppelganger, and thank you for meme-ing with me every workshop night. You are all I dreamed of.

To Qualia Reed. If every writer had a friend like you, no writer would ever condemn themselves to silence. Keep writing, keep being you.

To all who doubted me: I win.

Finally, I would like to acknowledge you, my readers. I am a storyteller. But what's a storyteller without listeners? Thank you for giving this story a chance.

Here's to many more stories, and many more chances!

S. L. Phanes

S. L. "Xander Phanes (they/them) is a trans non-binary
Arab American artist, author, and multimedia
storyteller. They are enchanted by the power and the
experience of stories through different
media. Their work consists of fantasy/science fantasy, and
their stories explore the mystery of the soul,
intersectional identities, the natural world, and our
relationship with it.

Don't be strangers! Connect with Xander on
Instagram @mxphanes

www.ingramcontent.com/pod-product-compliance
Lightning Source LLC
Chambersburg PA
CBHW030005010826
48973CB00009B/2669